# Me-YEOW!

## Book 4 of the Sea Purrtector Series

by *Jeanne Foguth*

# $\mathcal{A}$cknowledgements, $\mathcal{E}$tc.

Xander de'Hunter is a tribute to Rom, my 'greatest cat ever'. I am sure many of you will disagree because you know a certain feline, who is so far superior that s/he is surely 'the greatest cat ever', so perhaps it would be more accurate for me to say that Rom was the greatest cat I ever knew. Rom passed away at the age of 16.5 and had an amazing talent for using technology (we used to think he was a feline 007). Since this is a tribute to Rom, Xander de Hunter's skills with technology are exceptional, as is all of Catamondo, a world I never imagined existed, prior to writing The Red Claw.

*Me-YEOW!* is dedicated to the memory of Spooky Pilch, who was a fine house panther that went over the rainbow bridge this year (2016).

Many thanks to my faithful beta readers: Ellen, Marcha, Braden, Kaj and Paul without whom my work would have 'rogue commas' and 'renegade spelling', not to mention strange formatting anomalies. Thank you also to Kiara Graham for creating *Me-YEOW!*'s cover.

Cataloging in Publication Data is on file with the Library of Congress.       ISBN: 978-0-9913339-1-2

# Books by Jeanne Foguth

**Sci-Fantasy**

Kazza's Chatterre Trilogy:
*Star Bridge*
*Thunder Moon*
*Fire Island*

**Fantasy**

Xander's Sea Purrtector Files:
*Latitudes and Cattitudes* (Short Prequel)
*The Red Claw*
*Purr-a-noia*
*The Vi-Purrs*
*Me-YEOW!*

**Contemporary Suspense/Romance**
*Deadly Rumors*
*Fatal Attractions*
*Passion's Fire*

*C*hapter 1

*X*ander watched Mischief paddle her bogie board across the calm, shallow waters of the Caribbean Sea. Abruptly, his apprentice plopped down, nose touching the water, as she stared into the depths. The coral heads were easily visible, here, in the Rosario Islands, so he was sure there was plenty for her to watch. Hopefully, she got her fill because as soon as the marina had an opening, they'd haul Whispurring Winds out at the shipyard in Cartagena to paint on her hull and repair the damage Hurricane Catarina had inflicted on her mast and spars. Meanwhile, he and his apprentice would fly to India.

India.

He shut his eyes at the dreaded thought.

Over twenty-four hours in his travel crate was not something to look forward to, no matter how luxurious and excellent its technology or how much he enjoyed curling up in a good box. The idea of a full day in his crate made his seal point fur quiver. When he'd tried to express his misgivings to Merlin, his best pal hadn't understood. Apparently, Merlin's trips were short and mainly on charter flights or in Elegant Eats' corporate jet, so he had no clue how the average cat traveled. Even more annoying, though Merlin planned to meet them in Mumbai, his travel plans revolved around his marketing campaign and the promotional tour he was doing for his newest flavor, so he would be making shorter hops and have plenty of other things to do in between. Meanwhile, he and Mischief would make the trip too, but in two long consecutive flights and never leave their crates. By the time they rendezvoused with Merlin in Mumbai, India, they would have made trips of a similar length, but Merlin's journey would take a month, while he and Mischief would do it in an uncomfortable day.

Xander's tail smacked the cockpit's royal blue cushion in frustration.

A quick glance confirmed that there was no one close enough to observe him, so he made no effort to mask his feelings about the upcoming trip. He'd been trying to figure out a way to avoid further involvement with the Moreau mess since Merlin's research indicated there could still be two DNA freaks on the loose. Hadn't he endured enough when he dealt with Chester, Damon and those Vi-Purrs? Why did Merlin – and now, the Council - think it was his problem that a couple of those lab experiments might still be alive on the other side of the world? In the past few months, Merlin kept finding more evidence of the Moreau misfits – all in India and until last week, Xander had been able to avoid involvement. But, now Mischief had graduated and Merlin was determined that they would meet him in Mumbai and jointly deal with the last crumbs of the Moreau affair. In fact, Merlin had made travel arrangements for them all to meet in Mumbai. Unfortunately, Merlin had used the time to continue researching and he kept adding names to his list, so, now there weren't just two names on it; there were six cats, who might be part of Chester Moreau's sinister plan to take over Catamondo. The good thing was that all of them were in India.

The bad thing was that India was on the other side of the world and one of the listed cats was a Purrtector, so Catamondo's Council didn't want the investigation to go through normal channels.

Worse, the Council agreed with Merlin and had declared that anything related to the Moreaus was part of his investigation, so he and Mischief needed to go to the other side of the world – Mumbai, to be precise, because Sari, Mumbai's Purrtector, had been feral when the Moreau experiments had taken place in her Purrtectorate and she was on Merlin's list... He and Fluffy had confided in Sari, when he initially realized there was a link to India and he'd thought she'd tried to help. Had she merely prolonged his investigation with half truths and used his trust to find out what he knew? Xander's pristine seal-point fur threatened to stand on end and his claws itched to shred Whispurring Wind's cushions, but his extensive training gave him the control he needed to resist digging his claws into the royal blue canvas.

To take his mind off Sari and her potential duplicity, he focused on Mischief, who was now sprawled on her bogie board, face in the water and batting at something. Xander shut his eyes and shook his head. Why had he ever assumed he would obtain a purrfect apprentice if he could begin training her when she was six weeks old? He sighed. At least, she'd finally realized how important her education was and graduated with honors. His tail swished with the suspicion that she had only gotten good grades in order to get those surfing lessons Merlin had promised as a reward.

He stood up and shook himself. Watching Mischief waste time, which she should be using to prepare for their trip, was also wasting his time.

Xander went into the salon to Skype Merlin. Seconds later, his best buddy's emerald eyes were studying him. "Hey Pal, what's up?"

"Just floating around in the doldrums, waiting to haul out. Which means that I'm catching up on reports." His nose wrinkled.

"And your adorable apprentice?"

His tail slashed with frustration. "The Tadpole is on her bogie board watching fish and Hathor knows what else."

Merlin's ears perked with interest. "I'd take her bogie board over your reports any day."

Xander coughed to cover his growl of disgust. Of course the white Norwegian Forest Cat would purrfer that; he loved getting wet, too. His eyes narrowed to slits. "I have to deal with reports from my Purrtectorate."

"I have to deal with reports from my Purrtectorate, too and I also have tons of boring stuff to do for my job at Elegant Eats. The current marketing campaign is taking up a lot of time I'd rather spend surfing and napping.... I can't tell you how much I'm looking forward to taking two weeks off!"

Xander clamped his jaws shut, so he couldn't say how much he dreaded the coming vacation.... not because he would be seeing Merlin, but because of the length of the trip and the prospect of flying. He'd done enough air travel during his younger years on Catamondo's Kick-boxing Circuit to know that he didn't like airplanes. Of course, there was also the fact that they would be dealing with another piece of the mess Chester Moreau had created. The fact that the genetic misfit was still giving Catamondo problems from the grave, was nearly unbelievable. It was also unfortunately a fact.

Xander's tail thumped the settee.

Outside there was a big splash. Merlin's eyes widened. "Did she fall in?"

Xander snorted. "More likely she dove in."

"Shouldn't you check?"

He sighed and nodded. "I'll be back in a minute." Not wanting to waste time, he sprinted onto deck and hopped on top of the captain's chair, which had an excellent view of the now-empty bogie board. He narrowed his eyes as he searched for a certain troublesome calico and quickly spotted the tip of her tail sticking up in about two feet of water. Narrowing his eyes, he saw her front paw batting at a fat red starfish. When his thoughts darkened, he recalled Merlin saying, '*All work and no play...*' so shook off the negativity that continually plagued him over his apprentice's water obsession.

Mischief popped up for a breath of air, waved at

him, then with a laugh, dove back to spar with the starfish.

Xander went below to assure Merlin that all was normal – or at least as normal as it could be when living with Mischief.

Merlin raised a shaggy white brow. "Is the starfish any good at fisticuffs?"

Xander shook his head. "Though you'd think five legs would be an advantage."

"An extra leg should at least offer a bit of a challenge." Merlin shrugged. "Did you hear that the Counsel is being cautious about the information they share with Sari?"

Again, Xander shook his head. "I'm not surprised... if I were in their position, I'd be doing the same thing." Xander scratched his ear and studied his best friend. Merlin liked to pretend he was a big, beautiful, brainless beach bum, who just happened to be the spokescat for delicious gourmet food, but he was actually very well-read and smart. Merlin was also infatuated with Purrsident Mitzi Montgomery's purrsonal assistant, Cheyenne, so his interest in tracking down Moreau clones and misfits could be because Merlin wanted an excuse to contact her. Of course, there was also the possibility that Merlin had the ambition of being noticed by Catamondo's ruling cats. After all, he wasn't getting any younger.

Neither of them were.

So it was a good idea to keep an eye open for possibilities where one could be useful, even if – when – they got to be a certain age.... and Merlin was seventeen months closer to that age than he was.

Xander swished his tail as he realized that despite Merlin's obsession with Cheyenne, he also had a valid point that needed an honest answer. "While I don't intend to tell her anything about my real investigation, I plan to give Sari the benefit of doubt, until we can prove her guilt or innocence. It isn't anyone's fault if they have bad luck or live in the wild without proper documentation for a while."

"Figured that's the way you'd want to play it." Merlin's emerald eyes gleamed with approval. "While I don't plan to share any state secrets, I'm going to consider her innocent until she is somehow proven guilty.... Think the kid will have any problem pretending all is well?"

Xander shook his head for the third time. "I've only mentioned Gandharvas and Ganas' names, since they seemed the most likely to be DNA freaks or clones. No need for her to know that our hostess' name is also on your list of cats to investigate."

More splashes, closer this time, told him that Mischief was climbing the ladder onto the stern. "Sounds like Tadpole is done playing," he told Merlin, then he called for her to come below and tell Merlin hello. Her white, charcoal and gold fur was soaking wet, but her leaf-green eyes were sparkling with happiness.

"Fall in?" Merlin asked. She shrugged. He grinned. "On purpose?"

She giggled. "Would I do that?"

"If you're anything like me, you would."

Mischief gave Merlin a dazzling smile. "I wish other toms shared your enlightened opinion." She glanced at him out of the corner of her eye, then turned her full charm on Merlin.

Though Xander was tempted to box her ears, he knew he was older, smarter and more skilled, so he refused to allow her veiled insults to annoy him. Ever since he had been named the first Sea Purrtector, Xander had believed that Merlin would have been the ideal Sea Purrtector, but his pal had made sure that everyone thought he was just a gorgeous white Norwegian, who was the ideal representative for gourmet food. Only a select few knew about the water skills, which would have made him the purrfect Sea Purrtector. Listening to Merlin and Mischief chat about their plans to surf, when they finished vetting the suspicious cats, Xander wondered if Mischief and her water obsession was another example of fate. After all, water skills were something Sea Purrtectors should have. Right?

"Does the Council often contact you?" Mischief asked, riveting Xander's attention back on their conversation. What had he missed and why did Merlin look like he had an exciting secret?

"Yes, what did they contact you about?" Xander asked.

Merlin swallowed. "I'm not supposed to say, but since you'll soon find out, Lord Purrmetheus- "

"The one that's the head of the Council?" Mischief asked.

Merlin nodded. "Purr is a purrsonal friend, so we don't just chat about problems."

"I won't tell," Mischief said.

Merlin's gaze jumped back and forth between them, then, as if making up his mind, he leaned close to the screen and whispurred, "Purrsident Mitzi's health has become an issue." Mischief gasped. "Apparently, she has thyroid problems and might need to step down." Merlin glanced over his shoulder, even though no one else appeared to be in the room with him.

Xander's gaze narrowed on his best pal, who was obviously trying to avoid eye contact. While he was certain that Merlin's information was probably something he'd heard from the Council, the longer his pal kept his attention elsewhere, the more convinced he became that there was some other secret – an even bigger one – that he wasn't sharing. Could the Council be considering appointing his best friend Interim Purrsident?

He hoped so.

# Chapter 2

*T*he plane dropped so fast that Xander's stomach stayed somewhere far above. He closed his eyes, dug his claws into his crate's royal blue blanket and held on. A heartbeat later, his travel-crate smacked down on the floor, then bounced twice before it stayed in place. By the time the plane leveled off, his ears were popping and his his tail was as fat and fluffy as Ginny's feather duster.

"Did we crash?" Mischief howled, from her adjacent travel-crate.

"No." Since there was no one in a position to witness his reaction, he made no effort to camouflage his wild fur. "Apparently this pilot feels the need to hit every air pocket."

"What's an air pocket?"

"Not all air is equally capable of holding up a plane."

"Huh?"

"It's a term for ordinary turbulence."

"Whatever that was, didn't feel ordinary to me."

Xander closed his eyes and inhaled, held his breath for the count of ten, then blew away his fear and frustration. As his seal point coat began to relax into place, he said, "Think about how the surface of the ocean is usually cooler than nearby land -"

"You mean in the heat of the summer?"

His ears flattened at the interruption. "If that makes you happy." He remembered to breath. "Do you remember learning that warm air is lighter than cool air?"

"Heat rises; cool settles."

"Exactly! And when a plane flies over the ocean, the air above it usually has a different temperature, from the air over land. Some air isn't as good for holding up the wing-" The plane dipped, again, but thankfully, only for a second. Still, his claws vainly grasped for something secure to hold onto. Closing his eyes, he prayed to Hathor. This flight to Mumbai, India had only begun, but it already seemed to be a lot longer than advertised.

"Warmed air goes up," Mischief meowed. "Cooled air goes down. When we hit one of those air pockets, do you mean the air is cold and that's why the plane falls down?"

He took another calming breath. "Sounds like an interesting theory, but I don't know for certain because I've always heard that cold air is stronger because it is denser. You should use your collar to research that."

"I forgot my new one could use the satellites."

"This trip is a fine opportunity for you to get accustomed to its functions." The garish hot pink collar, which was her graduation gift, had only arrived the day before. Knowing Mischief, she hadn't even read the owner's manual; but he also suspected that she was techno-savvy enough to find the embedded user instructions.

"What about... never mind... I can figure out how to link it to the crate's backup power."

Dare he hope she would now be quiet, so he could try to relax? After a few moments of steady droning through the air, he loosened his grip on his blanket. When the plane continued to drone on straight and level, he clicked his own collar so he could make a check list of the things he wanted to get done, if they didn't crash on route. But first, he checked the weather; just because it was mid December and hurricane season was past, didn't mean that storms were smart enough to understand that they weren't supposed to happen in December. And just because pilots had licenses didn't mean they were smart enough to avoid storms.

As if to taunt him, the plane dipped a wing.

Was the pilot competent?

Was this plane safe?

"Why are you asking me?" Mischief meowed.

Oh, dear Hathor, he'd spoken aloud! This flight had him even more rattled than he thought. "Never mind."

"Never mind! Now, you've got me worried. Do you really think this plane is safe or not?"

"I think it is purrfectly safe."

"Are you sure?"

"Yes!"

"Are we almost there?"

He tapped his collar. Barely an hour had passed and the entire trip would take a day. "Of course not." This was already the longest day of his entire life.... he hoped he could survive another twenty-three hours.

"I still don't understand why we have to go to Madrid, first."

Xander sighed and explained, again, "Planes travel specific routes and there was no direct flight to India from Columbia – we were lucky to get space on this charter flight."

"Well how come we couldn't sail? It would have been much nicer than being stuck in these crates forever."

While that was certainly true, it wasn't practical. "One: Whispurring Winds's mast needs to be repaired and her hull needs to be repainted." His apprentice knew all this, so why bring it up? His ears flattened.

"Couldn't that be done in India? Ms. Ginny says things are more economical – that means cheap – there."

Xander inhaled, held his breath for the count of ten, then exhaled. "It is a very long way and if we had sailed, the most direct route would be through the Red Sea, which has pirates... I, for one, am not willing to jeopardize you, Mike, Ginny or our dear Whispurring Winds to high-jackers. Besides, in the long run, point two is that it is more economical to fly and it certainly takes less time."

Mischief made a rude sound then muttered something about it being ridiculous for a Sea Purrtector to fly, when they were obviously meant to sail.

"Tell you what, since we have a lot of time, you can write a paper comparing the time, financial costs and dangers between sailing and flying."

She said something even ruder about not needing to write more papers now that she'd graduated. He rolled his eyes upward, because he liked to think Hathor was up there, watching over him. Hadn't his self-absorbed apprentice ever noticed how many reports he wrote for his job?

His thoughts were disrupted when Mischief snarled, "This whole thing is just dumb! If we must fly, how come we're flying East-North-East, when India is just plain East?"

"That's because the plane is chartered to go to Madrid, first." He paused, then decided to give her something to think about, "Plus the plane will need more fuel."

"You mean we're way up here and don't have enough fuel to get where we need to go? Is the pilot nuts or just dumb? And YOU! You knew we left the ground without everything we needed? What's wrong with you? Don't you ever put me in a position like this, again!"

"We're fine." He figured saying it aloud might make it so. For certain it felt good to hear the words and he certainly didn't want to attempt explaining how planes only could carry a certain amount of fuel or that the more they carried, the heavier the plane became, which meant that it needed more power – meaning more fuel – to fly. No matter how many times Merlin had brought up the subject, while planning one of his own innumerable sales trips, the mathematics of how weight affected a plane's purrformance baffled him.

"You're confusing." She growled. "Do you try to blur facts on purrpose?" She sounded the way he felt when Merlin meowed about the topic.

"No."

She snorted. A moment later, the plane hit another pocket. "We should have sailed," she wailed.

"A plane can take a more direct route and go a lot faster," he said, claws as firmly anchored as possible. "If we'd sailed, our route wouldn't be as direct because we'd need to stay on water. This trip is about nine-thousand-two-hundred-miles, believe me flying is better. Just think about how fast this plane is moving -"

"And how fast might that be?"

As the plane hit another air pocket, his stomach fluttered, but fortunately, his crate didn't leap into the air. "I'm not sure of the precise speed, but planes travel very fast, probably around four or five-hundred-miles per hour." Hopefully, this flight stayed on route and didn't fall to the ground – or ocean - or whatever made the worst splat.

"Whispurring Winds is fast and a lot more comfortable."

"More comfortable, yes, but with a good wind and the help of the motor, we only averaged about ten miles per hour. SO IF we sailed at our top, average speed twenty-four hours per day and had nothing slow us down, it would take us over a month to get there. By plane, the trip will just take a day. So, sailing isn't as fast as you think." Xander's tail smacked his crate. "Furthermore, when I say it would take Whispurring Winds a month, my estimate assumes we would have good weather, make good speed and didn't get shot by pirates, eaten by alligators or whatever other hazards might be possible on such a long trip."

"You're such a pessimist."

He growled, "Realist." Taking another deep breath, he tried the counting trick, again. After exhaling, he added, "I don't have the luxury of taking a month to get there. Sari says those cats have symptoms suspiciously similar to bird flu."

"SO?" Mischief growled. "Why do WE need to help her? Seems to me she should have asked someone who was a good veterinarian. And, lest you think you're good at doctoring, let me assure you that you most certainly are NOT. You're not even a good patient."

How dare she bring up his recent annual check up! "If this is part of the Moreau situation, I need to be there."

"Oh, please, you know that all those tainted toys were destroyed. How could her problem possibly be part of that?"

"For one thing, we don't know if the shipment

we discovered was the first one. Thousands of toys could have been shipped before we discovered the problem." The plane felt like it fell at least fifty feet before his crate bounced back into place and the pilot regained control. What was wrong with this flight?

"So you really think that flu situation could be part of the Moreau mess?"

"Would we be flying to help Sari sort this out, otherwise?" Dreadful as this trip was, he never wanted to set paw on another plane for the remainder of his nine lives.

Mischief sighed. "Probably not." Her claws drummed an annoying cadence on her crate, but at least she wasn't tapping coded insults, which she'd done since starting to learn it. "You said that Ms. Sari is Mumbai's Chief Purrtector, so how come you jump when she says that she thinks an epidemic is breaking out in Ma-har-ash-tra?"

"Mumbai is a huge city, which is located in the state of Maharashtra."

"So they have two names for the same place."

"Basically."

"Do you have to make things so complicated?"

Xander sighed. "I don't... I wish I knew all the answers and if there are still Moreau creations out there, but I don't and I need to find out. I also wish I knew, for certain, if a shipment of Chester's toys somehow managed to get delivered."

"Is that why Mr. Merlin said he'd meet us there?"

"Partly, but I think he is mainly bored and thinks

this will be a big adventure."

"Because of Ganas and Gandharvas' birth records?"

Xander nodded, then remembering that she couldn't see him said, "If they are actually Moreau creations and they are as strong and devious as the others have been, it will be good to have his help. Plus, you and Merlin had a deal. You fulfilled your part, I intend to carry out our part." If he'd realized the promise of surfing lessons as a graduation gift would inspire her to change from a student who was barely getting by, to an exceptional scholar, he would have bribed her the moment he'd recommended her adoption. Of course, on day one, he hadn't had a clue that she had a water obsession and loved wet sports. Who could have anticipated that?

"Do you think there is good surfing in India?" Her hopeful tone at the thought of learning to surf from one of the best in Catamondo was typical. How had he ended up with a best friend and an apprentice who both loved water? He shook his head over the perplexing situation. "I have no idea. You should research surfing as it relates to India."

"I hope Mr. Merlin likes me. I mean, I know he likes talking to me on Skype, but in person is different."

Xander looked up at the royal blue ceiling of his travel crate. "He likes everyone." She made a doubtful sound. "I'm serious. It's one reason he is such a good spokes-cat."

"But obviously, he doesn't like being that."

"Why do you say that?"

"If he liked his job, why would he stick his whiskers in this Moreau mess?"

Xander blinked. Had his apprentice just spoken a truth or was his theory about impressing Cheyenne Merlin's real motive? He might never know the answer to that; for certain, he wouldn't at the moment, so he reverted to what he knew was fact, "We had a deal: you study hard, get good grades and graduate and I would do my best to give Merlin the opportunity to give you the surfing lessons he said he'd reward you with. So, of course I understand why that's the main thing on your mind. But now that I think about it, since he knew how well you scored in your exit exams and wanted to meet us there, it stands to reason that there must be good surfing in India." Mischief howled with delight. He sighed. "I need to focus on my job and finish my to do list... and to do that, I need peace and quiet."

"You think you'll find peace and quiet in this bumpy, noisy plane?" She howled with laughter. "Good luck!"

He could see a corner of her bright pink travel crate out of the side vent of his own. Water sports were not the only thing that mystified him about his apprentice. Her current love of that glaring shade of pink was just as purrplexing. Still, it sort of suited her. "No, I don't think this plane will ever provide peace and quiet, but it would be nice if we tried, so not another word out of you."

Though she didn't utter another syllable, he heard her claws tap -.-- Y --- O ..- U .-. R . E

How many times had he told her not to use

contractions when tapping Morse Code? Xander shook his head, certain that he knew what was coming next. -- M . E .- A -. N Her claws tapped. Yep, he'd been right. He should be used to hearing her opinion of him and be able to ignore it, since whenever his apprentice heard something she didn't like, she told him he was mean. Didn't she realize that he wanted the best for her and was trying to educate her? Give her the tools she'd need when she became a Purrtector? So, yes, she needed to learn reading, mathematics and history, so the bad things didn't get repeated.

Mean would be hurting her physically or saying hurtful things for no reason. Trying to teach her how to take care of herself was not being mean. He took a breath, with the intention of giving her a piece of his mind, then realized that if he did, she would win her little Morse Code game.

Dear Hathor, why had he taught her that annoying form of communication? To Mischief's credit, despite the occasional coded insult about his character and her increasing dislike for planes, she didn't actually utter another word, until they landed in Madrid. Then, she had plenty to say, but he ignored her. Fortunately, once they were airborne for the second leg, she was so quiet that by the time the sound of the plane's engines subtly changed or when there was a solid thud from underneath, which he learned was the landing gear locking into place, he had begun to worry about her... Not enough to break his own silence, but enough to feel a muscle-weakening rush of relief when he saw her calm calico face.

# Chapter 3

As their crates were unloaded, a humid breeze brought a sour smell combined with a sickeningly sweet scent, which the odor of fuel and sweaty bodies did not improve. Please Hathor, don't let this whole country stink!

Mischief asked, "Is this another stop for fuel?"

"We have arrived," he said, while trying not to breathe.

"Are you sure? I mean, it seems just as hot and humid as Columbia and it smells the same, too – just awful."

A cautious sniff brought the vile combination of sweat, exhaust, dead mouse, rotting fish and over-sweet flowers. Xander made a sound of agreement. Did all airports stink like this or was it just ones in tropical areas?

"Is it hot and humid everywhere?" she asked.

"No.... Would you rather the epidemic was in some frozen place?"

"It might be nice. I mean snow and ice look pretty. And it's almost Christmas. From what I've read, Christmases are best when they're white, which means snow and that's pretty unlikely when it's this hot."

His mouth dropped open for a full half minute, before he tasted something rancid and snapped it shut. By the time they'd passed through Customs and Immigration, he realized that Mischief's understanding of winter apparently came from pictures, movies and song lyrics. For her, ice was something to cool down drinks and play hockey with, when a stray cube landed on the floor. She had no way of knowing how snow could suck the heat out of one's bones and leave them feeling miserable. Sleet was the worst, but she would probably love it, since she adored everything that was wet.

As soon as they emerged from Immigration, Sari, a chestnut-colored short hair, wearing an ornate gold collar and the gaudiest harness he'd ever seen jingled her way toward them. Despite her dreadful attire, Xander moved toward the side of his crate, where she pranced next to her chauffeur, the tiny bells on her collar and leash jingling like a miniature sleigh. After greeting her, he stayed as close as possible to her because her scent was like an orchard of blooming oranges, which was better than anything else that he'd smelled since landing. Her chauffeur placed their crates on a low, flat cart, then Sari hopped on the cart for a ride while her chauffeur pushed it to the parking garage. Between jingles and chimes, Sari told them how happy she was that they had arrived safely. Once they got to the car, her chauffeur ushered them into the backseat of Sari's plush, tan sedan, then he stowed their crates in the trunk. Finally free, Xander was able to give Sari the appropriate head butts and cheek rubs. Up close, he realized the scent of oranges was mixed with other spices. His mouth watered. As they got comfortable on the soft tan leather seats, the chauffeur started the engine and turned on the air conditioner.

"Is your weather always like this?" Mischief asked.

"Today is typical." Sari looked Mischief up and down, paying a lot of attention to her simple-looking hot pink collar.

The chauffeur extracted the comfortable car from its parking slot while other humans rushed to and fro in no obvious pattern. A palm tree's trunk blinked red and green and several white stars glowed on some shrubs, but Xander couldn't be certain if those were Christmas decorations or not.

"Do they have any good surfing around here?" Mischief asked.

Sari blinked twice, before she turned her confused expression on him. "Is surfing involved with this disease?" Her ear twitched, causing her collar's bells to jingle. "To the best of my knowledge, none of the cats who have fallen ill have been anywhere near the beach." She scratched her ear, which set off all her chimes. "For that matter, with the exception of the cats who are employed at the wharves and on boats as rat catchers, I can't think of any that go near the beach and I have only heard of one of those who showed the flu symptoms."

Xander's ears perked. "Was he or she one of the first to fall ill?"

Sari shook her head, again the gold bells on her ornate golden collar tinkled. Could the cat move without making music?

Mischief looked from Sari to him, "Do you know when Mr. Merlin will arrive?"

"He arrived late last night." She swished her tail in dismissal. The scent of orange overpowered everything else. Had she dipped her tail in orange essential oil or something?

Eyes watering from the intense aroma, Xander blinked. "I'm surprised that he didn't come with you to meet us."

"He needed to do stuff for his job and will meet us for lunch." Sari batted a golden tassel hanging from her fancy silk harness; the movement made all the sequins and gold bits glitter as the bells chimed. Mischief's eyes widened as if she hadn't noticed the ornate harness before, which wasn't all that surprising, since Sari's leash and collar were both made of gold links and had all sorts of do-dads and tiny tingly bells hanging to distract one's attention. The thing reminded him of a charm bracelet, which he'd seen a human female wearing. Somehow, Sari's yellowish-green eyes and chestnut fur seemed to go with the flashy leash and garish harness and Sari managed to make the ensemble look sort of elegant.

As the vehicle made a sudden lunge forward, he slid across the tan leather seat, slamming his shoulder against the door; meanwhile Mischief ricocheted off the back of the seat and landed on the floor. "Sorry about that," Sari said. "I should have warned you that Tamil's driving can be a bit erratic when we're in crowds."

Mischief hopped back up and looked out the window. "There are lots of people here. Is this usual?"

"This city is home to over eighteen-million humans," Xander said. "Didn't you research it like I told you to do?"

Mischief's tail bristled. "Of course I did. I just didn't expect everyone to be at the airport." Sari began to laugh, but managed to camouflage it with a fake sneeze that made all her bells ring. Mischief's eyes narrowed. "You think I'm funny or just dumb?"

"I think you are unfamiliar with this city." The vehicle jerked in a spurt of speed accompanied by honking and bad words by the chauffeur. With a yowl, Mischief slid against the back of the seat. Meanwhile, Sari appeared unfazed by the erratic ride. "I guess I should have warned Tamil to take it easy." She gave a delicate shrug. "Since you live on a boat that moves with the waves and since Merlin had no issues, I assumed your balance was excellent."

"It's the unexpectedness of his driving, not a balance issue," Mischief growled.

Sari gave his apprentice a gentle smile. "Of course it is, dear."

Mouth flat, Mischief didn't say another word for several miles, but his acute hearing detected her nails tapping out very unflattering opinions of their hostess, her chauffeur, her jangling harness and India in general. Lest Sari notice and understand the code, he involved her in a discussion of the details about the potential epidemic and keyed his collar to record and analyze what she said. The more she shared, the more his stomach twisted with the certainty that a crate of tainted toys had somehow gotten to its destination. Their discussion was interrupted when her gaudy gold collar chimed. Sari put her paw to it and said, "Sorry, but I need to get this.... Hello, Ahmeda.... Oh, good. Do you think he could bring an assistant or two?... No, no, not for me, for a couple of my guests, who could really use a good grooming." Her critical yellowish green gaze traveled over Mischief, then moved to him. Xander glared at her. Flustered, Sari quickly concluded her call.

Xander kept his tone calm and ignored the fury blazing in Mischief's eyes. "I am sorry if our grooming offends you, but it was a long trip and a significant portion of it was turbulent."

Sari inhaled, "I understand that, but surely you want a good brushing before this evening's benefit." Her eyes narrowed on the blue sapphires circling his throat. "Your collar could use a good cleaning, too." She turned her attention on Mischief. "A hot pink collar is a bit garish for such a formal event, we'll see what we can do to make you presentable – all the best cats will be there."

Mischief's nose began to match her collar, but instead of verbalizing any of the insults she'd been tapping out, she simply asked, "What event?"

"Didn't Merlin mention it?"

Xander ears flattened. "I did NOT travel twenty-seven hours – one of which had horrid turbulence – to attend some ridiculous fund raiser and have you show off your supposed connections to 'all the best cats'." Xander hissed. "And I am so sorry that the color of my apprentice's collar offends you, not to mention that you think my own needs cleaning, but what earthly business is it of yours?"

Sari sat up straighter and raised her chin. "Your grooming is perfectly fine for traveling and I certainly understand that, but surely you do not expect to attend Merlin's event without proper grooming."

Oh, so now it was Merlin's event. Xander snorted. "I came here to investigate your report of a possible epidemic." He lowered his voice and spoke slowly, "Do you have a situation here or not?"

"Of course I do."

Xander raised a brow. "But you also think I should waste my time and go to some high class event."

"All the best cats will be there." Sari simpered, as if overly proud to let him know that she was part of the elite crowd. "It will be an excellent opportunity to gather more information."

Mischief growled. "I will have you know that I earned this collar as a graduation gift. It's super high-tech and it's even water proof!"

"That's very nice, dear, but it is hot pink."

Mischief's tail whacked the leather seat. "And your collar is gaudy gold. How is that better than my pretty pink?"

Though her coded tapping had informed him of

exactly what she thought of Sari's outfit and several other things, he was surprised to hear her verbalize her thoughts aloud. And while he knew that he and his apprentice were both thinking of the damage Chester Moreau had intended to do with stolen fur, Sari was still supposed to be innocent until proven guilty. Mischief's claws tapped that she would like to strangle Sari with her ridiculous collar. Neither of them needed that, so Xander gave her the sign to back down. Mischief opened her mouth, then snapped it shut and though anger still blazed in her eyes, she turned her back to Sari and began watching the passing scenery and quit tapping out her opinions.

"Sorry about that. I'm afraid we are very tired and cranky from our trip."

Sari inclined her head. "Apology accepted."

Mischief turned her head to glare at him. Xander bit his tongue and again, gave Mischief the sign to back down. She shot him a venomous look, but complied. By the time they got to Sari's condominium, which overlooked her Purrtectorate from the thirty-third floor of a thirty-six floor tower, he couldn't decide if the ride from the airport or the turbulence had been the worst part of his trip. For certain, Sari's intention to have him groomed rankled and made him suspicious that she might have ulterior motives.

Had Merlin been right when he added her name to his list of cats who might be Chester Moreau's clones? If so, it would certainly explain why she didn't have the sense to avoid bells, which gave her presence away to prey.

And it would certainly explain her desire to get her paws on their fur and collars.

## chapter 4

Merlin showed up later that afternoon. Sari continued to act as uptight and phony, as she had since Mischief insulted her, Merlin and Xander did the appropriate head-bumps, then were still so happy to see each other that their reunion devolved into a short wrestling match, which offended Sari so much that she left. Mischief began snickering, so he quickly introduced his apprentice to his best friend.

Merlin's smile warmed his emerald eyes, "Pleased to finally meet you in the fur!"

Mischief's nose turned brighter than her collar as she studied her toes. "I'm pleased to meet you, too." She glanced up, then quickly turned her attention back to the way her dainty white paws looked on the gaudy oriental rug. "Mr. Xander talks about you and Ms. Cha-cha a lot."

"Oh, so you talk about my flaky sister, too?" Merlin's ears perked and laughter danced in his expression.

Xander shrugged. "I explained how you and I met."

"When you taught him to swim and surf," Mischief said. She peeked up at Merlin. What was wrong with his apprentice and why was she acting shy? "Do you know if there is good surfing here?"

Merlin laughed. "India has 4,349 miles of coastline. While most of it hasn't been explored with the intention of locating surf spots, you know there must be some great waves when the conditions are favorable. And once this... possible epidemic... and the origins of a couple cats is sorted out, you and I will find some good waves and see if you like surfing."

Mischief smiled bigger than he'd imagined possible."How about Diego Garcia Island?"

Merlin's brows raised. "For a first lesson?"

Mischief eagerly nodded.

"Where is Diego Garcia Island?" Xander asked.

"In the middle of the Indian Ocean, just barely above sea level," Merlin said.

Xander's ear twitched. "Unless my collar is wrong, Mumbai is by the Arabian Sea and The Bay of Bengal is on the other side of this country." His tail slapped the colorful carpet. "Just because we're in India doesn't mean we're close to the Indian Ocean."

Merlin laughed, then turned his attention on Mischief. "You've researched this, haven't you?"

She eagerly nodded. "It has some of the best surf on the planet!" Her eyes gleamed and she began to bounce with excitement. "If you're half as good a surfer as Mr. Xander says, I thought maybe that might be why you chose to meet us here." Then she frowned and took a step toward him. "For your information, the Indian Ocean is just South of here." She took another step. "You told me to research things. I did. AND apparently I did a better job than you, since you didn't realize that." With a decisive nod, she turned back to Merlin and had the nerve to bat her little lashes. "So, Diego Garcia Island?"

"Probably not for a first lesson," Merlin said.

Mischief deflated.

"While I don't want to get between you and your vacation plans, we're here to figure out if there is an epidemic or if it's just a coincidence that an illness with similar symptoms sprang up in this area." His tail swished. "Did you find out anything, yet?" he asked Merlin.

"Wish I had, but-" Merlin shrugged, then sighed. "The main thing I noticed was that this country's wealthy live very well, but the majority live in squalor. The ones, like Sari, who have a good life, seem to think they are superior, while the slum dwellers are focused on survival." He frowned. "It's sad and I don't know how to help." His tail whacked the rug. "I came here on a promotional tour to debut our new flavor to everyone, not just the financially fortunate."

"Really?" Mischief meowed. Xander understood her doubt, since he, too, had always considered the Elegant Eats brand to be exclusively for the 'financially fortunate'.

Merlin inclined his head. "Pumpkin Purrfection

is for vegan cats and my sponsors thought India was an ideal place to promote it."

"Vegan as in vegetarian?" Mischief asked, eyes huge. Merlin grinned and nodded. "Vegetarian!" Mischief blinked rapidly. "Are you saying that cats, here, are vegetarians?"

"Many of them have staff that are vegetarian... Have you noticed any cows roaming around free?"

Xander nodded. "As a matter of fact, I have. What's with that?"

"Oh, I know! I know!" Mischief gave him a superior look. "Some of the religions here think cows are sacred. You'd get in more trouble for hurting a calf than a human child. But what I don't understand is how come it's not against human law to do bad things to cats." Mischief growled. "And now you tell me we need to eat vegetables!"

Xander laughed. "You loved the pumpkin pie our chef made for Thanksgiving. In fact, as I recall, you ate nearly half a pie by yourself."

Her nose colored. "I would have eaten it all if Ms Ginny hadn't caught me."

"Many vegetables taste good," Merlin said, "and I assure you that I would not support anything with kimchi, okra or cauliflower." He shivered. "However, pumpkins have a high-fiber content that makes it good for any cat suffering from constipation. It also helps with upset stomachs and indigestion. And it is an excellent source of Vitamin A, starch and fiber. Yams, are similar to pumpkins, but sweeter..." He stopped talking when he noticed that Mischief was looking at him as if he'd grown a second head. "Sorry about that, I've been doing a lot of promotion, for Pumpkin Purrfection in the past few months."

"Understood," Xander said. He looked around to make sure no one else was in ear-shot, then lowered his voice, "What is your impression of Sari?"

"Nouveau rich."

"I think Mr. Xander is asking you if you think she might be one of Chester's puppets or purrhaps a clone." Mischief glanced at him. "That is what you meant, isn't it?"

He nodded. Merlin's expression became thoughtful and guarded as he focused his attention on his apprentice, "What makes you wonder about her?"

"She wanted to groom me and thinks my collar is tacky!" Mischief's fur stood up for a moment before she controlled her feelings.

Xander cleared his throat. "Actually, she wanted to have someone come in and groom both of us and 'clean' my collar." Since he didn't want Mischief to realize that Merlin already suspected Sari, Xander added, "Don't know about you, but after seeing how that Moreau bunch was trying to undermine Catamondo by growing fakes, I don't trust anyone who is unknown to groom me or touch my collar."

Merlin nodded in understanding. "If those Moreaus had taken some of my fur to get my DNA and planned to clone me, then kill me after my look-alike replaced me, I'd be purranoid, too."

Purranoid? Him? Xander's ears flattened and he started to shake his head but Mischief growled,

"Sari said, 'A hot pink collar is a bit gaudy for such a formal event, we'll see what we can do to make you presentable – all the best cats will be there.' Is my collar's color a big deal or was she just being rude or was she just trying to get her paws on it to download my data?" Mischief's tail smacked the oriental carpet. "AND, THEN she said, 'Surely you do not expect to attend Merlin's event without proper grooming.' What's wrong with my grooming? I mean, I spent 27 hours – HOURS, not minutes – in my travel crate and I think I look pretty darn good under the circumstances."

Merlin wrapped his impressive white tail around her, like a comforting hug. "You look fine. It's just that some individuals seem to think that in order to make themselves feel important, they need to criticize others. It never works in the long-run and they tend to be miserable souls."

"Without true friends," Xander added. He tilted his head as he studied Merlin. "Do you think Sari has a purrsonality problem and her plans to groom us was an attempt to feel important or superior?" It could make sense, since he and Merlin both had ranks far superior to hers and that could be intimidating. Merlin's rank of Co-Continental Purrtector had even had Mischief talking to the rug for almost an entire minute. In the distance, the soft chiming of small bells began to move closer.

Merlin frowned in the direction of the jingling sound. "It is possible," Merlin said, "but it's also very possible that your suspicions could be correct. I mean, what cat wears falconry bells?"

Xander blinked rapidly. "Are you certain that's

what they are?" Merlin nodded. "I didn't realize that birds wore bells, just thought it was very strange for a cat to wear so many."

"Is tonight's hoity-toity event really yours?" Mischief asked.

"If you mean the benefit to raise money for free clinics, yes." Merlin scratched his ear. "If you want to come, you're fine as you are, but if you'd enjoy a good brushing, you're welcome to come to my suite and have Cynthia groom the travel off... and I would make certain she disposed of any fur properly."

"Cynthia?" Xander raised a brow. "Is she the groomer you had three years ago?" Merlin's smile showed fangs, as he nodded. "In that case, unless you think we'd reveal too many of our doubts to Sari by leaving, I'd like to take you up on that offer."

Merlin stood up. "Leave Sari and her possibly tender feelings to me." He tilted his head toward the door. "Go on up to the penthouse, while I deal with Jingle-bells. I'll tell her I need your assistance and we'll meet her at the gala." With a decisive swish of his impressive white plumbed tail, Merlin moved toward the sound of approaching bells.

Xander and Mischief hurried in the opposite direction.

# *C*hapter 5

*T*he benefit was crowded with cats of every shape, color, age and size, but they all shared the ability to pay for the opportunity to be there and many took more time than necessary to preen as the catarazzi photographed their arrival. Xander had no desire for his photo to be in *The Daily Mews*, where it could alert Chester Moreau's cohorts about his location, so he sat behind a large flower pot containing a tropical plant with huge green leaves and studied Sari as she worked the crowd. Something about her movements and ability to stay in front of cameras reminded him of Lucy Fur, whose relationship with the Moreaus would probably always leave cats wondering if she'd been a Moreau puppet or defector. Xander hoped that now that Chester was dead, any reasonable cat would avoid anything to do with Chester's plans to undermine Catamondo, but one could never be certain. If Sari had ever been involved with the Moreaus, now that she was a respected Purrtector, she could try everything in her power to counterbalance Chester's evil plans by doing good – even if she did try to do that in front of cameras. One main difference between Sari and Lucy Fur – aside from their loyalty being unknown was that Sari not only attempted to hold visual attention, her continual tiny movements created an audio distraction.

"You'd think this was 'her event' instead of Mr. Merlin's benefit, wouldn't you?" Mischief whispurred. "I mean, look at her, she's treating everyone like they're her guests, but Mr. Merlin said that she's *his* guest, just like we are."

"We're in her Purrtectorate. She's used to being in charge, here." Xander said, his gaze on Sari's glittering gold collar. Whenever the attention of those in her immediate vicinity seemed to wander, her small movements and the resulting jingling increased. Had he ever met any other cat so desperate for attention?

Doubtful.

"Do you really believe that?" Mischief's whiskers quivered and her eyes sparked green fire, or purrhaps it was just the light reflecting in her eyes. "You and Mr. Merlin are a lot more important than she is, so she shouldn't try to act so important."

"Purrhaps that's why she's trying to stay in the spotlight." Or purrhaps this was normal behavior for her. Only time would tell which theory was right.

"I think Mr. Merlin is right and she's a nasty 'nouveau rich'." Mischief's claws tapped out an even more insulting name, which Xander chose to ignore.

"I only know what the files say about her, which isn't much. That's why I'm watching her." He didn't add that he was also trying to determine if her bells were doing more than keeping attention on her. Though he doubted it, there was a possibility that bells, like claws, could be used to transmit messages. The question was why she would need or want to do that.

"Well, if you ask me, it'd be better to hear what she's saying, not just watch from a distance and listen to that jangle." Mischief leaned closer and whispurred, "Do you think she noticed that Merlin's staff moved our travel crates so she couldn't snoop in them?" With that, Mischief ducked under a huge leaf and began to zig-zag her way through the gathering in the general direction of Sari.

Xander stayed right where he was and studied Sari's body language, which had become subservient to a huge tom, whose fur had a purplish cast. Exceptionally large cats were something Chester and his doctor produced and Damon's eyes had been purple. Xander involuntarily shivered before he regained his self-control. That color fur was rare, though not unheard of. The tom's steely gray eyes looked normal, too. The most baffling thing was Sari's behavior. Why was the self-centered number one cat in this city behaving like she was a lowly servant to the big purplish tom?

"Why are you hiding behind this philodendron?" Merlin whispurred.

"I'm observing, not hiding." Merlin raised a brow. "Do you happen to know who the big old guy with Sari is?"

Merlin laughed. "My furiend, Purr a.k.a. Lord Purrmetheus. And you'd know him, too, if you paid as much attention to Catamondo's rolls as I need to for marketing."

The name rang a vague bell, but not enough to put a history with the tom. Xander keyed his collar to provide the missing information. "How'd she convince India's Top Purrtector to come?" He hadn't realized she had that much influence, though he had heard that Lord Purrmetheus had been voted Head of Catamondo's Council. Merlin was right, he should pay more attention to the political aspects of his job.

"Jingle-bells didn't invite him." Merlin snickered. "I did. It was a good marketing move." Ah, that explained a lot. The big old guy turned his head and the same green that Merlin and Fluffy wore flashed at his throat. If he'd seen that, previously, it would have answered a lot of questions, before he displayed his ignorance to Merlin. His pal nudged him. "Come and meet him. He's a great guy and his mate is really nice, too." Without waiting for a reply, Merlin ducked under the massive green leaf and made a bee-line for the huge cat.

Xander followed, but stayed far enough back so he could observe everyone and their reaction. When Sari spotted Merlin, she perked up and gestured for him to join them. Amusing, since that was exactly what his pal planned to do. Then, Sari said, "Lord Purrmetheus, may I present-"

"Fraser, old chap, about time you showed your whiskers!" Purrmetheus said, effectively interrupting Sari's introduction. Next, Purrmetheus gave Merlin cheek rubs, left, right then left again followed by a friendly head-butt. "I've been looking forward to testing your new flavor since you told me about it. Took you long enough to get it to market."

Sari looked from Purrmetheus to Merlin then back and forth three more times. Finally, realizing they not only were acquainted, but were ignoring her, she pretended to see someone the next group over, so she jingled a step away. If Xander hadn't been so suspicious of her, he might have felt a bit sorry for her. However, he didn't consider social climbing an attribute, so he didn't waste any time worrying about her feelings. Instead, he wondered how Merlin knew Purrmetheus and where on Earth they'd met.

"Purr, I'd like to introduce you to-"

"Kamikaze Xander d'Hunter. As I live and breath, it's you in the fur!" Before he knew what was about to happen, Purrmetheus was giving him the same exuberant greeting he'd given Merlin. As soon as the head-butt landed, Purrmetheus said, "I've never seen anything like that video of you fighting that dreadful chupacabra-vipurr-creature. Absolutely amazing fight. Must have watched it a hundred times. Amazing. Absolutely amazing. I admit that I wondered what the Council was thinking when they appointed you to be our first Sea Purrtector." He patted Merlin. "Always figured Master Fraser would have been our best bet, but after seeing that fight, I've been totally confident they made the purrfect choice. Amazing fight. Simply amazing."

Xander forced a congenial smile and wished Lord Purrmetheus didn't have such a loud voice and hadn't brought up the incident that had plastered him on the front page of *The Daily Mews* for weeks. It seemed like every eye within twenty feet was staring at him; Merlin's expression was amused, but most were merely interested or inquisitive. Except for Sari, whose glare could singe fur. Didn't they understand that he was trying to keep a low profile?

"Very pleased to meet you, Lord Purrme-"

"No need to be so formal, I'm Purr to my friends and I certainly would like to consider you my friend."

"I'm honored." Xander dipped his head. "How long have you known Merlin?"

"Well, my dear friend, that is a rather long story, but the short of it is that after years of skyping, Frasier and I met last year in London."

Sari's glower turned into a phony smile, then she turned, vibrating her bells, back to her new group and began telling them a story, in a voice that was louder than was quite appropriate. Merlin tipped an ear in Sari's direction and raised a brow. Xander gave a slight shrug.

"And who might this be?" Purrmetheus asked.

Xander glanced over his shoulder. "This is my apprentice, Mischief de Hunter."

"Enchanted to meet you, my dear," Purrmetheus said in his booming voice. Xander wondered if the old tom might be a bit deaf or if he liked to be the center of attention, as Sari obviously did. "I'm surprised that your apprentice doesn't have a blue collar," the old tom added. "Not that the bright pink isn't lovely, but I thought the Council designated blue for the Sea Purrtectors... Er, rather, Sea Purrtector, since thus far, we only have you."

Xander nodded. "Mischief recently graduated from the Academy and is officially my apprentice, but not a Sea Purrtector – yet. Since she's always wanted a pink one, I didn't see any harm in her wearing pink before her rank locks her into blue."

"Quite right." Purrmetheus nodded. The big tom curled his tail around an elegant elderly lady, whose coloring was suspiciously similar to his. Was purplish fur more common on this side of the world? He narrowed his gaze on the individual hairs, but no matter how closely he looks, their fur appeared to be typical except for the odd color. "My mate, Lady Violet Tiyos." She leaned lightly against Purrmetheus as the official introductions were made, then gave them each cheek rubs, left, right then left again followed by a gentle head-butt. Was this their standard greeting or some local ritual that his files hadn't mentioned?

"I'm so pleased to meet all three of you," Lady Violet purred, then she spent extra time fussing over Mischief, who proudly explained the functions of her new collar. "My furiends call me Vi." She gave Mischief another friendly head butt. Beyond them, Sari's expression suggested that either she'd had a mouthful of something rancid or she was very upset about not being in their group, which the three highest ranking cats in the room – probably in the country of India. Her expression had changed when Lady Violet gave his apprentice purrmission to use her intimate name. Could Sari have risen to such a high rank and still have some sort of inferiority complex? Though he already knew Merlin's concerns, his pal had never mentioned why he'd added Sari to his list of possible suspects, so Xander keyed his collar to research Sari's background in detail and see if there might have been any changes or strange gaps, which could indicate that Chester had somehow substituted one of his creations for the real Purrtector. Even as he made the note, he realized jealousy and pettiness were not something confined to Chester. Yet he couldn't quite get past the way Sari had tried to get samples of their fur and it certainly didn't hurt to make certain Mumbai's Purrtector was doing a proper job — particularly when his own job had taken him into her Purrtectorate.

Was there really an epidemic, or had she used that as an excuse to lure him here as some sort of revenge thing for ruining Chester's evil plans?

Merlin expertly maneuvered Lord Purrmetheus away from the females and closer to Xander then lowered his voice to ask, "By any chance are you familiar with Ganas and Gandharvas?"

The big tom blinked then, matching Merlin, lowered his own voice, "They are well known in Hindu mythology; Ganas are various types of supernatural beings that serve Lord Shiva, though Ganesha, the elephant-headed god, is actually their boss. Gandharvas are male nature spirits who are many things but the ones I've heard of all seem to be singers and musicians. A Gandharvas character is mentioned in both Hindu and Buddhist mythology. Thus mythology would be something both names had in common... I had no idea you were interested in that." Due to the lowered tone, Purrmetheus' voice was now at a normal level.

Merlin swished his tail. "Ganas and Gandharvas are two toms, I heard about. I didn't realize the names had any historical significance."

Lord Purrmetheus' posture stiffened and his attention zeroed in on Merlin. "If they're related, I would assume their parents had an interest in mythology."

"Entirely possible," Merlin shrugged. "May I assume that those names haven't been flagged for inappropriate conduct?"

"Not that I've noticed, but I will purrsonally ask each of my Sub-Purrtectors."

Merlin waved a dismissive paw. "Don't make a big thing out of my curiosity." Since Merlin was taking that stance, Xander made certain that he appeared to be scanning the crowd and indifferent to their conversation.

"Might I ask why you asked?" Lord Purrmetheus asked.

"I overheard those names earlier and thought the toms discussing them sounded... apprehensive." Merlin shrugged, as if it wasn't important. "Just curious," he repeated.

Was it his imagination or did Lord Purrmetheus relax when Merlin didn't push the subject? If he hadn't figured it would be pushing his luck, Xander would have taken closer look at the big tom's fur, instead, he had his collar access the official file on Lord Purrmetheus and Lady Violet. Interestingly, while both were listed as Russian Blues, there was no note about unusual purplish tint. In fact, silver-blue was listed as the official fur color on both on their pedigrees and their documents didn't have any of the tell-tale anomalies Merlin had noticed in Ganas and Gandharvas' paperwork. Had Merlin been testing the older tom with his question, or was he actually as paranoid as Xander had felt since meeting Chester Moreau? It wasn't normal not to know who he could trust and it certainly wasn't a comfortable sensation to wonder about every new face and even wonder if those in high rank might be Chester's genetic substitutes.

Even from the grave, Chester Moreau was still affecting his life. Xander breathed in, held for a count of ten, then blew out his worries.

Xander gave himself a final mental shake, then tuned into the conversation Merlin and Purrmetheus were having about a trip the Lord Purr planned to Nepal, which was where his pedigree stated that he and Lady Violet had been born. Clicking on his collar, Xander discovered that Nepal was located in the Himalayas and bordered to the north by China and to the south by India. Himalayas? A quick click confirmed the Himalayas were the highest mountains on the world. If it hadn't been for his extensive training, he would have shivered at the idea of heading someplace like that in winter. Still, any country that named its capitol Kathmandu, must be a good place. As one part of his conscious absorbed the streaming information from his collar, he also listed as Purrmetheus told Merlin that he'd wanted to go to Nepal earlier in the year, but had needed to stay and officiate at the Diwali festival, which apparently was a big thing and ran for five days and then he'd wanted to stay for this benefit, so he could see 'his dear Fraser'.

Loud laughter erupted from Sari's group. Looking their direction, his gaze passed over Mischief and Lady Violet who appeared to be enjoying each other's company, but the contrast between his apprentice's pristine white, black and gold fur and the elderly dame's purplish coat was disconcerting. Could the high elevation and cold explain why Lady Vi and Lord Purr had strange fur? If so, he thanked Hathor that he'd been born at a lower elevation and had a purrfectly normal seal-point coat.

Mischief's howl of mirth brought his attention back to the unlikely pair. Lady Violet was laughing right along with his apprentice and just beyond them Sari looked like she'd eaten rancid mouse droppings. Whatever the ladies were laughing about had to be more fun than Lord Purrmetheus' planned trip. Xander casually maneuvered around Merlin and asked, "Care to share the joke?"

Mischief said, "Did you know that a lot of humans think Ganesha is a god?"

He blinked at the unexpected question, but quickly covered his confusion. "As I understand it, humans have hundreds of names for their gods and while I've never heard that one, I admit that I've always wondered why some of them get upset about it, while others understand that '*a rose by any name would still smell as sweet*'."

Lady Violet and Mischief both giggled until their eyes teared. Some days, trying to be charming and quote supposedly important human literature simply was not worth the effort.

Mischief wiped her eyes. "The name wasn't the funny part." Xander put a question mark in his tail. "It's what humans think he looks like." He smacked her with his tail. "He's an elephant-headed god! Can you imagine?"

"It's typical for other species to have gods that look totally different from Hathor."

"I know that, but think about it. This is a human god and you know what size they are, right?" He nodded. "Well, I didn't say Ganesha was an elephant, which would make sense, I said that Lady Vi said he's the *elephant-headed god*... that head would be way bigger than a human and you know how Mike says that people who think a lot of themselves have a swelled head." She burst into laughter, again.

He turned to Lady Violet. "How in the world did you ever get on the topic of religion?"

She shrugged.

Mischief sobered. "Mr. Merlin was talking about Ganas and Gandharvas and mythology and that got us talking about weird things that some humans -"

Lady Violet cut in, "Actually, most species have some odd beliefs. But what I actually said was that the only Ganas I'd heard of was the one in Hindu mythology and he was a kind of supernatural being in Shiva's entourage, but Ganesha, the elephant-headed god, was his boss." Lady Violet's gray eyes twinkled with merriment. "Mind you, that is all I know about the name and I'd never thought how silly a god that was just a big fat head would look." She giggled.

"I heard of a tom named Gandharvas," a big, stocky black cat from Sari's group said as he moved halfway between the groups. "He is supposedly a nasty one."

"How come I've never heard of him?" Sari asked as she jingled position so her circle now included the three of them, plus the stocky black cat.

"He's from Nashik and I only heard about him because my staff buys their grapes, there," the black cat said.

Why did that sound vaguely familiar? A quick tap of his collar provided the information that Nashik was a city in the northwest region of Maharashtra and was near the western edge of the Deccan Plateau, which was a volcanic formation. But the most interesting part was that the river had been dying due to pollution created by factories. But fortunately it had been cleaned. Fluffy had mentioned that the chemical factory Dr. Isla Moreau worked at had been fined for pollution...

Xander casually asked Sari, who was now making continual tiny movements, which resulted in constant ringing. "Isn't Nashik where the Moreaus lived?" Her eyes widened in surprise, then she nodded with a discordant jangle of noise. He smiled. "That's why it sounded familiar." He watched her out of the corner of his eye, as he turned back to Lady Violet and asked, "Do you know if elephants also consider Ganesha a deity?"

"I've never asked, but to be honest, I've never actually had a conversation with one, either."

"Oh, I thought there were several in this country."

She nodded. "True, but none have ever been seen in my high rise and, to be honest, I prefer to stay home."

Why had she felt the need to say 'to be honest' twice? Wasn't she normally honest? Knowing that he needed to say something, Xander said, "Interesting."

Meanwhile, Lady Violet ignored the fact that Sari had maneuvered herself to include them in 'her circle', by leaning close to Mischief. As she began telling her about her favorite hobby: bird watching, Xander hoped his apprentice didn't return the intimacy and extoll the joys of water sports. As Lady Vi droned on about fight characteristics, he glanced at Sari. Why had she wanted to be involved in this group and why had she looked so relieved when he dropped the topic of Nashik? While he was wondering why, there was also the disturbing question of why Lady Violet had said 'to be honest'... Previously, when he'd met cats that used that phrase, they had eventually proven to be dishonest, so it made him wonder if those who said, 'to be honest' were so focused on the perceived honestness of their remarks.

For certain, before the evening was over, he planned to find an opportunity to chat with the black cat without Sari around and find out what, if anything, Ganas had to do with fruits and vegetables. Fortunately, this proved quite easy to do because the speakers chose that moment to announce that the buffet was open and everyone was urged to try all the flavors and leave their opinion. With a loud discordant jangle, Sari rushed to the laden table as if she was still the starving feral cat, which her files claimed was the life she'd been born to. Xander's ears perked. "Guess she's really hungry."

The black cat snorted. "More like she wants to be first in line because she thinks the catarazzi will photograph her and being first makes her seem more important."

"History tells us that important individuals had testers eat first, to see if the food was poisoned." Xander cocked an eyebrow. "I'm Xander de Hunter."

"Kamakazi, everyone knows who you are." The big black house panther butted him, giving him a close look at his tasteful gold collar, which designated the wearer as the Chief Purrtector of a large area and meant the tom held equivalent rank to Sari. "In fact, if there are any cats on the planet that can't recognize you it's because they're blind or just plain ignorant." The black tom must have been able to read his confusion over that statement because he added, "Your fight with that chupacabra-wannabe was riveting. Don't know anyone who hasn't watched that clip at least a dozen times."

Xander willed himself not to shiver at the near-death memory or wonder why this was the second time within an hour someone had brought up his battle with the Vi-Purr. Trying to appear nonchalant, he asked, "Are you from Nashik?"

The black cat's amber eyes showed surprise. "No, that's just a bit Northeast of here and the land is very good for growing fruits and vegetables."

"Commander Whiskers Killmouskie! 'Bout time you got here! Are you ready to eat pumpkin?" Lord Purrmetheus boomed a moment before he gave the black cat unrestrained cheek rubs, left, right then left again followed by a friendly head-butt. Greeting finished his steel gray gaze turned to Xander. "Has Killmouskie been telling you about our planned trip?"

Xander shook his head.

Lord Purr head butted the big house panther. Now that he knew the tom's name, it seemed vaguely familiar. The tom had amazingly long whiskers, which begged speculation on whether whiskers was a nickname, like his own Kamakazi or if his whiskers had been impressive since birth. "Killmouskie is Purrtector of the Land of the Gods."

The black cat's nose flushed. "Uttarakhand is the actual name of the state... it's in the northern part of India." Commander Whiskers Killmouskie turned his attention on Lord Purrmetheus. "Uttarakhand is occasionally referred to as the Land of the Gods because my state has many Hindu temples and pilgrimage centers."

"Uttarakhand is known for its natural beauty because of being close to the Himalayas, which is where Lady Vi and I come from." Lord Purr added. He tail smacked Killmouskie in the manner of long time friends. "You going to be ready to head North tomorrow afternoon?"

"Of course."

"Care to join our party, Fraser?" He raised a purplish eyebrow to Merlin.

"Wish I could," Merlin said, "unfortunately, I've got a couple more days of PR to do here, before I'm officially on vacation."

"Now dear, don't forget that I want to stop at the market in Nashik for grapes, onions and tomatoes," Lady Vi said. *Grapes, onions and tomatoes?* His shock must have shown, because Lady Violet gave him a warm smile. "Don't worry, Kamikazi, I'm not planning on poisoning anyone. That particular market is known to have the best produce in the country... I believe it has something to do with the volcanic soil they have in the area." She shrugged. "Regardless, have no fear, I don't plan to serve it to any cats... In light of our treaty with Dogdom, I don't even plan to serve any dogs." Her tail swished in such a way that he wondered if she might have a history of poisoning dogs."To be honest, our offspring's staff love eating those revolting things and never display any ill effects."

"Trust me," Lord Purr said, using another catch-phrase that brought Xander's attention to high alert, "humans seem capable of eating those things without any negative effects. In fact, I've heard some of them claim that grapes and onions are healthy. Imagine that!"

Xander blinked. Though his chef swore that red onions were full of amazing vitamins and other good things, like being blood purifiers, she knew these were only safe for humans, not cats or dogs. Grapes were just as bad for pets and he'd known some cats who had developed major kidney problems and worse from innocent looking snacks, prepared by ignorant staff.

Killmouskie snorted. "Were they referring to grapes or that nose-curling stuff they brew from them?"

"Never thought to ask," Lord Purr boomed.

Several heads turned to see what their supreme Purrtector found so amusing, but Sari's expression was the only one that held fury. What was off about her? The more he watched Sari, the more he understood why she was on Merlin's list of questionable cats. Unfortunately, there was still no proof of her being a Moreau creation; the only things for certain were that she had an unfortunate need for attention and trashy taste in couture.

Mischief sidled up to him and whispurred, "Ms Vi invited me – us – to go with her to Ut-tar-ak-hand." When she tried to pronounce the word, it sounded like she was gagging. "And then to Nepal, it's up in the mountains, where there is snow. Can we go?" Her big leaf-green eyes begged him to say yes.

"Have you forgotten why we're here?"

She shook her head.

"Would you give up your surfing lesson to see mountains?"

Her whiskers drooped.

"I didn't think so. But I'll tell you what, I'm willing to make a deal."

Her eyes narrowed. "What do you want me to do and what do I get out of it?"

"I want you to put our reason for being here first and for that I'll meet you halfway, so you'll get to spend some extra time with your new furiend. Do we have a deal?"

Her eyes narrowed as she studied him. "How much extra time? She is very interesting and so cool. I mean how many cats do you meet who are cool enough to tint their fur purple?"

Xander blinked. "She told you she tints it?"

Mischief eagerly nodded. "It's part of the formula for her shampoo and it's really good for repelling bugs, so that's why she started using it, but I think purple fur is beautiful. Don't you?"

He blinked several more times. "I hadn't thought about it, but it's not objectionable and it's certainly better than feathery fur or bright red fur."

"Do you ever think about anything besides work?"

Xander sighed.

"What are the two of you whispurring about?" Lord Purrmetheus boomed.

He smiled as he turned toward the big tom. "Your lady invited my apprentice to travel with her to Uttarakhand."

"Excellent idea!" Lord Purr beamed. Sari scowled.

"We were negotiating a compromise," Xander said. "We came here at Ms. Sari's request to help figure out an illness she'd had reports of, so solving that is our priority."

Killmouskie looked around and focused on Sari's enraged expression. "What sort of situation do you have?" he asked as he headed toward her.

For a brief moment, shock rippled through Sari's expression, then she gave Killmouskie a huge smile and began loudly meowing about the Nashik District's Purrtector asking HER for assistance. Xander's ears trembled at her high-pitched tones, but he had to give her credit for explaining the issue to Killmouskie without giving away any classified details.

Merlin nudged his attention back to Lord Purrmetheus as Lady Violet stepped into the space vacated by Killmouskie. She twirled her whiskers. "Well, does your delightful apprentice have your purrmission to accompany me?"

"Alas, we came here to help Sari determine if an epidemic might be starting. She's only had a few cases here in Mumbai, but she believes the infected cats came from the northwest region of Maharashtra – probably the Nashik Division."

"Nashik is the third largest city in Maharashtra and 14th most populous city in India," Mischief said, proving that she'd done some research. "And in a city that big, he'll need my help, but I'd really, really love to see your mountains."

While he didn't want to appear inept and incapable of following the lead on his own, if Nashik was anything like Mumbai, he could use all the help he could get – particularly if there were tight places or other nasty parts, like some spots he'd already seen from the car. "My dear Lady," he told Lady Violet, "I'm honored that you enjoy my apprentice's company so much, but if she is ever to wear the blue, she needs to complete her training. I'm sure you understand."

Lord Purrmetheus gently head bumped his mate. "We can not interfere with the education of such a promising apprentice, but since my duties have already put us several days behind schedule, I don't see why we couldn't spend an extra day or three while you choose the ideal gifts in Nashik." He turned his attention on Xander and lowered his voice. "Purrhaps I could even offer the Kamakazi some assistance with introductions, accommodations and such?"

Xander bowed. "That would be appreciated."

"It is settled then! You and your charming apprentice will travel northward with us, tomorrow afternoon."

As Lord Purrmetheus told him about their plans to take the Panchvati Express, which was apparently a train, Xander stole a quick glance at Sari, to gauge her reaction to this development. Fortunately, her focus was centered on Killmouskie and she was talking so loud that he doubted she could hear anyone but herself. However, he could hear Lady Violet telling Mischief how pleased she was that they would at least be able to visit low mountains, together.

"Low mountains?" Mischief asked.

"Compared to the Himalayas, where I as born, *all* mountains are low," the lady said with a laugh.

*Chapter* 6

As the train's brakes squealed, Mischief raised her head and looked at Lady Violet, who wasn't reacting to the noise or changing velocity. Mischief then turned her attention on Lord Purrmetheus and then Killmouskie. Last, her attention focused on him and though he was certain he hadn't moved a hair, which would let her know he was watching her through his lashes, he suspected she knew that he was also trying to decide if this was their stop. Since no one was getting up, he hoped this was just another stop on the overcrowded train and they didn't need to get ready to depart. Xander took a deep breath and began counting to ten, so his frustrations could bond with the air he blew out.

Mischief's claws began to tap, "When you told me we were taking the Pan-cha-va-tea Express, I figured it would be fast, like a plane, except keep its wheels on the ground. That is what express means, right?" She rested her chin on her paws and glared at him, effectively muting her tapping.

Why did she blame him, when Lord Purrmetheus was the one who'd made their travel arrangements? He'd merely gone along with the plan because it got him where he needed to go and he didn't want to waste valuable time figuring out this country's transportation system. Detestable was too nice a word for this over-crowded train with its horrid whistle and bumpy ride. If they hadn't been up most of the night, the trip might actually seem interesting. Unfortunately, between the plane trip and the benefit, he was way behind on sleep. The banquet had lasted late into the night, then instead of resting, Sari's soap-opera-reaction to the news that they were heading to Nashik required that he give her attention. Xander was so tired that it was a struggle to keep his whiskers from wilting, so he simply shrugged. Mischief's glare deepened into a glower, then she began tapping her claws in a discordant pattern. He had a reputation to maintain, so he couldn't afford to behave like a cranky kitten. Besides, who could compete with Mischief?

Purrhaps he should copy Lord Purrmetheus and spend the four and a half hour trip dealing with correspondence. Xander fought back a yawn and wished he could use the trip to find a sun puddle to nap in, as Killmouskie and Lady Violet had done the moment they boarded the train at Mumbai Central Station. How many times had they made this trip before they were able to take the sights, scents and sounds for granted? And how could anyone manage to sleep over the screech of those brakes, which seemed to happen at least twice an hour?

Mischief's claws returned to tapping out complaints about the train, then stopped after stating that this express train stopped at ten stations during the journey. How had she managed to get a sneer into the word express while doing code? She concluded that this express trip would take 275 minutes total. Seriously? Since when did any schedule post the total minutes? Or was she so bored that she was concocting a math problem?

If her information about the ten stops was accurate, how come she'd looked like she expected everyone to hop up and get ready to disembark? Worse, since this was only the third stop, it was going to be a long, long, long day. Perhaps he should follow Lord Purrmetheus' example and deal with his correspondence. If he accessed his voice mail, he could still watch the country click by. With a sigh, Xander sprawled in a sun puddle and activated his collar. Boring as some of the messages were, they weren't being tapped in code. Good as his plan was, shortly after the train resumed its northward trek, exhaustion and the rhythmic motion relaxed Xander enough to doze off. Twice, the changing motion and screaming brakes woke him enough to open an eye to see if Lord Purrmetheus looked like he was preparing to disembark. The next time he woke, the sun puddle had vanished and the electric lights were on. It was noticeably cooler and his sensitive ears told him they were at a much higher elevation. Lord Purrmetheus was turning off his tablet and Lady Violet was fussing over Mischief, who looked confused by all the motherly attention.

Killmouskie was doing a series of graceful, yet powerful stretches, which were similar to the Tai Chi routine Xander had done each morning, since he was old enough to walk. Though he was accustomed to exercising in private, if it was appropriate for Whiskers Killmouskie to do his routine, it was fine for him to join in. With that thought in mind, he hopped up and began his own stretches.

=^.^=

Lord Purrmetheus ushered his party off the train on the opposite side from the station's platform. He'd done the same thing when they boarded and Xander had wondered why at that time, but now that he'd had the opportunity to see several boardings and unboardings, he accepted that Lord Purr was being very clever because individuals on the platform seemed to be carried by the crowd as they either boarded or got off the train. Voluntarily was much better. Massive herds of people were something new. Granted, in his old kick-boxing days there had been vast numbers of observers, but never so many humans. Was this country uniquely overpopulated or had he become jaded by living aboard a boat and spending so much time away from urban areas?

When Lord Purr stood still and looked around, Whiskers Killmouskie took charge with a, "Follow me!" and strolled purposefully northward. "I saw a map of the town and the railway is on the southeast side."

That was enough for Xander and the rest to follow Whiskers instead of risk getting separated as they wound their way through the teeming crowd near the platform. The farther he got from the station, the more relieved he was to have that stinky experience behind him, but the more he began to realize how huge this country was compared to the Caribbean Islands, where he'd concentrated most of his attention for the past year.

"It's kinda grimy here," Mischief said. When had she gotten next to him? Had he been that distracted by the exhaust from the train and other vehicles, not to mention his growing concerns about finding possible products of Chester Moreau's evil genetic experiments in a country, which was home to millions of cats?

"You mad at me for some reason?"

"No."

"Do you think the black dust is from the train exhaust or the volcano?"

"Does it matter?" He glanced at her. She was getting so tall that he barely needed to look down. When had she grown up? He gave his head a slight shake to rid his mind of the distracting thoughts.

She glared at him. "I was trying to figure out why everything was sort of grayish."

"Does is matter?" he repeated.

"Are you angry at me"

"No."

"Then how come you're acting so grumpy?"

"Thinking and hoping we didn't come here on a wild goose chase."

"They have geese here?" Her leaf green eyes gleamed with eagerness. "I've heard that stuffed goose is yummy!"

"That is an expression. I was saying that I hope we're not wasting our time."

"Oh." She padded along in blissful silence for a good five minutes, then as they approached a bus stop, she said, "According to my research, Nashik is next to the foothills of some mountains and it's almost a half mile above sea level, making it one of the highest cities in India, so if what you say about heat rising and cold going down is true, shouldn't it be warmer here?"

"Not necessarily."

Mischief growled. "Then how come you said it was so, when it's obviously cooler here than it was at Ms. Sari's, which was just above sea level?"

How could he explain this apparent discrepancy? Xander took a calming breath, then began, "Yes warm air rises. But it's also true that the temperature is three or four degrees Fahrenheit lower for every thousand feet higher we are. I once met a tom who loved springtime best and bragged about choosing the climate he wanted to live in by creating a formula based on temperature to altitude."

Mischief snorted. "How gullible do you think I am?"

Xander shrugged. "It's true. You see, the main place air is heated is at the earth's surface, where it is warmed by sunlight. So there are always updrafts of rising hot air above us."

"Wind does not go up."

"I'm not talking about wind, I'm talking about heat rising."

"You said draft, that's wind."

"I said updraft and that is a small current of rising air. If you take it in context with what I was explaining, I was telling you that warmer air goes up because warm air is usually less dense. I guess you could say that an updraft is less dense air rising until it reaches air that is either warmer or less dense than itself."

"Professor Meowingtons said that the higher we are, the less air pressure there is because the rising air is expanding." Mischief's tail swished in thought.

"That's a good way to describe an updraft. See, you already knew about this." If he could get her off this topic, he might be able to hear what Lord Purrmetheus and Lady Violet were discussing with such intensity. "Air is a gas and gases are cooled by expansion. So the draft of warm air that starts rising from the earth's surface continually cools itself as it rises, therefore both nature laws are true. Got it?"

"Purrhaps."

"Well, think about it for a while and I'm sure you will understand."

Mischief gave him a mutinous look. "Did you just tell me to be quiet?"

Xander raised a brow and grinned. "Purrhaps." Her nose wrinkled, as if she was smelling something worse than pollution, rotting garbage and unwashed humans, but she didn't say anything.

Everyone except Lord Purrmetheus sat down at the bus stop. When he cleared his throat as if getting ready for an important announcement, Lady Violet motioned Mischief to be quiet. "We will be staying at the villa of Countess Catula Mundalar, this city's Purrtector." His attention centered on Mischief. "She was very kind to extend her invitation, so it would be good to return the favor."

Mischief's eyes narrowed and she sat up straight. "What is the best way to do that?"

Lord Purr's harsh expression softened. "She is sensitive about her fangs, which are a bit longer than usual, so you can show kindness by not staring at them or making jokes."

Mischief raised both brows. "Is she a vampire or something?"

Lady Violet laughed. "You do come up with the funniest things."

"Well, isn't that why she's named Catula? Isn't it some play on the name Dracula? He was a human vampire with long fangs."

Lady Violet blinked in surprise. "I've never thought about it, but I'll bet you're correct. No wonder the Kamikazi wants you along to help him figure things out."

Mischief sat even straighter.

Xander bit his tongue.

"Well then," Lord Purr said, as a sleek red bus cruised to a stop, "this should be our bus. All aboard for Castle Tower on Gangapur Road."

Mischief hopped up with excitement. "We're staying at a castle? How exciting!"

"Castle Tower is the name of her high-rise,"

Lady Violet whispurred, as they settled on a vacant seat.

"Oh." Mischief sighed. "I knew something like that was too good to be true."

From across the aisle, Killmouskie said, "I'm sure you'll be much more comfortable there than in an actual palace... they're very drafty places and all too often, they are infested with snakes." His big black body shivered.

Her little calico face scrunched up as she studied the heavyset black fellow, who reminded Xander of an NFL linebacker. "So are you saying there are actual palaces and castles here in India?"

"I thought everyone knew about the Taj Mahal," Lord Purrmetheus said.

Lady Violet's eyes sparkled, "It's only about a thirteen hour train ride north of here. If you'd like to visit the palace, we could make a detour on our way to Nepal!"

Before his apprentice could respond, Xander said, "While that sounds like a lovely option, we really do need to investigate the illness that Sari told me about. If we do our job instead of turn our trip into a sight-seeing vacation, hopefully fewer will become ill."

Both Mischief and Lady Violet sighed, but indicated they understood.

Lord Purrmetheus curled his tail around Lady Violet. "The Council wouldn't have appointed the Kamikazi to such an important post, if he dropped the mouse at the first opportunity."

"I know," Lady Violet mumbled.

"I tell you what," Mischief said, "I'll send you pictures and notes of what I'm doing every day and you can do the same, then it'll sort of be like we're sharing our experiences."

Lady Violet perked up and Lord Purrmetheus looked at his apprentice with interest, but as the bus began to slow, he looked out the window. "We've arrived!"

Xander studied the Castle Tower building and wondered why it had been given such a fancy name, when it looked very similar to apartment towers all over the world. As they hopped off the bus, a gust of wind ruffled their fur. Mischief jumped, startled, then gave a self-conscious laugh and said, "Wind is the perceptible natural movement of the air, especially in the form of a current of air blowing from a particular direction."

Killmouskie laughed. "Didn't realize you were so interested in Earth Sciences."

"Oh, I am," she assured him, as she stepped onto the elevator. "Mr. Xander has been teaching me a lot about air. Did you know there could be pockets of less dense air that can make planes fall?"

The big black tom blinked several times. "A plane crashed at my local airport a couple years ago, but *The Daily Mews* said that was caused by wind sheer."

Mischief turned big questioning leaf-green eyes on him. "Wind shear is a little different from an air pocket," Xander said.

"Don't both make planes fall?" Mischief's expression dared him to disagree.

"If you recall, an air pocket is created when areas of air have different densities, so they are not equally capable of holding up a plane. Meanwhile, a wind sheer is a difference in wind speed or direction in a small area. And, instead of density, you literally have wind that can be described as either vertical or horizontal. Vertical is probably what caused the crash in Killmouskie's Purrtectorate."

Any further discussion on the topic ended when the elevator binged at the penthouse and a tiger-cat with impressive fangs was revealed by the opening door. Thank Hathor that Lord Purr had warned them about her teeth, otherwise, he might have thought some lab had gotten its paws on saber-tooth tiger DNA! Xander forced his fur not to stand on end and pasted a friendly smile on his face as Lord Purrmetheus stepped off the elevation and gave cheek rubs – left, right then left again followed by his signature friendly head-butt – to something comparable to one of Chester's mutants. As soon as Lord Purr finished his exuberant greeting, Lady Violet, then Killmouskie did the same thing. Mischief gave him a wide-eyed look and gulped. He knew exactly how she felt. At least he thought he did, then Lord Purrmetheus introduced them and with a meow of greeting, Countess Mundalar grabbed him and gave him what must be the standard Indian greeting. His stomach tightened and his tail threatened to flare. It was all he could do to keep his smile in place and his fur from standing on end.

Then, it was Mischief's turn. By the time Countess Catula was through greeting her, his apprentice looked considerably fluffier and her nose matched her hot pink collar. He gave her credit for having enough control to keep her fur from standing completely on end and was confident that by the time her apprenticeship was done, she would be in complete control of her emotions. "I'm so pleased to meet you," Mischief told her toes. "And it is so nice of you to invite us here."

Lady Violet laughed and wrapped her tail around Mischief. "Isn't she a dear?" she asked Catula. "Can you remember when we were her age and just as shy?"

"Indeed I can," Catula said. "Come in and have a snack. I'm sure the food they served on the train was typically boring and yesterday, a box of Pumpkin Purrfection arrived... I think this is a special enough occasion to open a few cans. Don't you?"

"Quite right!" Lord Purrseidon said.

Killmouskie and Lady Violet nodded. Had Merlin singled out Countess Catula Mundalar for a complimentary box or had Merlin had his marketing staff send boxes to multiple Purrtectorates so they could all participate in the previous evening's product introduction? If Xander was a gambling cat, he'd bet that all the main Purrtectors had received a similar box, which meant that Merlin's product launch could be much more complex and massive than he'd ever imagined. With that sort of organization and attention to detail, it was a miracle that he managed to juggle his work with Elegant Eats as well as be a first-rate Purrtector.

Or, purrhaps he'd merely sent a box here because he felt bad about not being able to come, himself, but that shouldn't have been necessary, since he'd agreed to check out the last three names on his list.

Xander swished his tail to reset its fur, then followed the others toward a lovely dining room with floor to ceiling windows that overlooked Nashik.

As they savored Pumpkin Purrfection, which was delectable enough to deserve the name, Xander watched the interplay between the Countess and the others, who seemed to completely accept her, exceptional fangs and all. As the conversation moved from topic to topic, he noticed that Lady Violet's body language was respectful toward both Killmouskie and Catula, but affectionate toward her mate and Mischief. Meanwhile, Lord Purrmetheus treated Killmouskie like a pal and Catula with... uncertainty, which was exactly how Mischief was acting. He felt hesitant about her, too, so tried to overcompensate by being overly polite.

Finally, the conversation turned to why he and Mischief had come to Nashik. Initially, Countess Mundalar's big gold eyes registered surprise that he had traveled over half the world to investigate a health issue that seemed to have begun in her Purrtectorate, then when the Moreaus were mentioned, Catula not only seemed to understand, but she become animated about helping them track down the information they needed to make certain there were no more freaks trying to undermine Catamondo.

Killmouskie frowned, "I thought you came here to find a couple toms named Ganas and Gandharvas."

Lord Purrmetheus' steel gray eyes narrowed. "And I thought he'd merely mentioned those mythological ones to have something to talk about." Pumpkin Purrfection forgotten, India's Chief Purrtector straightened up and studied him. Xander would have felt totally uncomfortable at being caught in a slight mis-direction if the tip of Lord Purr's whiskers hadn't held an orange glob of pumpkin.

Xander laughed as he ran a clean paw over his own whiskers. "What I heard about Ganas and Gandharvas made me think they might be some early DNA experiments and yes, I was somewhat concerned about them because of that. I am here to tie up any threads that are still open from the Moreau situation. So, yes, my original reason for making this trip was to verify if – or if not – the illnesses that Sari told me about were some form of the bird flu, which I know Chester Moreau planned to use to kill cats in this Purrtectorate."

"Why my Purrtectorate?" Countess Catula asked.

"That's simple," Mischief said, "he was angry that his laboratory here was shut down and he and his staff were thrown out of India."

For a moment, Catula's forehead furrowed in thought. "Since he wanted revenge just because Catamondo refused to accept him and his other... *creations*... I guess it isn't a big leap to see why he'd want revenge on my Purrtectorate for some other insult." She scratched her ear. "Do you really think Ganas and Gandharvas could be some of his experimental freaks?" She narrowed her eyes, which somehow made her already impressive fangs look larger. "Would he really have sent someone back here to wreck havoc?"

Xander swished his tail. "I won't know if they have anything to do with that until I've had a chance to investigate them." Since he seemed to have arrived at a point where it was wise to let everyone know why he'd come, Xander told them everything about the tainted toys that had been packed to ship to Purrtectorates, including this one, then he continued to honestly answer questions about Chester Moreau's evil plan and what he'd done to foil it, late into the night.

As the morning sun lightened the horizon, Countess Catula Mundalar took him to the window and pointed out the location of the closed Moreau laboratory. "I heard about it because of articles in *The Daily Mews*," she said, "but I'll check the records to see if my predecessor wrote down anything about them."

"Predecessor?" Mischief asked.

"I became Nashik Purrtector two years ago. Prior to that, Professor Puff-a-lump held the office."

"He resigned due to health issues," Lord Purrmetheus said.

Countess Catula nodded. "Kidney issues... smart as he was, he couldn't seem to remember to drink enough water."

Killmouskie snorted. "Everyone knows that we cats are eighty percent water, so we need that even more than humans, who are only about sixty percent water."

"Obviously, knowing something and remembering to drink are two different things," Mischief said.

Xander cleared his throat to get everyone's attention, then settled down to make a plan. By the time the sun was fully over the horizon and a wonderful sun puddle was taking over the dining room floor, they each knew what they would do to purrsue the investigation.... after a nice nap, of course.

# Chapter 7

The vibration of Xander's collar woke him. He hopped up, stepped over Mischief, then hurried into the next room and tapped his collar. "Yes?"

"Why are you whispurring?" Merlin asked. He explained that everyone else was still asleep. His best pal snorted. "How do you figure that you'll ever get anything done, if you sleep the day away?" Merlin gave a soft growl. "I've already organized crates of Pumpkin Purrfection to be delivered to fifty more kibble kitchens, posed for a dozen ads, bugged Jingle-bell's collar, eliminated two of the last three names on my list and responded to all the priority email from my Purrtectorate."

Xander blinked the sleep from his eyes. "Why the heck did you bug her collar?"

The pause in conversation carried the subtle sound of a paw being licked, then run over fur. Merlin said, "I'm making sure she's who she claims to be."

Cats used grooming to make themselves feel better during stressful situations.... Was his pal anxious about something or so overworked that he needed to multitask?

Xander's eyes narrowed as he inadvertently recalled how Sari had tried to get her paws in his fur and collar. When they had moved out, she had apparently realized she had upset him and she'd sent him so many messages asking why he'd left that he'd been tempted to put a block on her. Still, behavior that could simply be the result of ego, didn't explain what had motivated Merlin to do something that drastic. "And if she isn't guilty?" He didn't need to explain how the Council would view such an action.

"I'll cross that bridge if I get to it." Merlin didn't sound concerned.

Did his furiendship with Lord Purr provide him purrtection? If so, why didn't he say so? Could there have been a secret session that gave Merlin special privileges to verify Sari's allegiance? It was the only thing that made sense, but if that was true, why hadn't he been informed? He was officially leading the investigation, wasn't he? Something was off with this situation, he just couldn't put his paw on what it was. "Will you still be too busy to join us for a couple days?"

"'I'm afraid so." What was it about the way his buddy was phrasing things that made him feel that something he didn't know about was going on and that, for some reason, his investigative methods were being tested?

Where had that thought come from? Xander

gave his head a shake, then began his morning stretching routine, as he told Merlin the tentative plan, "Since I have two separate issues to check out, today, we will divide and conquer."

"Huh! I had the impression that Ganas and Gandharvas were staying together – just wasn't able to pinpoint exactly where from home-base."

"Mischief, Killmouskie and Lady Violet will look into their leads at the market, so hopefully I'll learn something to share, soon."

"And you'll be catching up on your beauty sleep?" Merlin teased.

"You didn't think I did this investigative stuff myself, did you?"

Merlin's laugh was loud and long as he caught the sarcasm, then he said, "Seriously, what's more important than investigating that pair?"

"The old Moreau Chemical Plant and talking to whomever remembers them and finding out if anyone stayed behind. I figure that Mischief knows Ganas and Gandharvas' names and that should be easier than trying to find information that may not exist."

"Valid point."

Was it his imagination or did Merlin sound impressed? Xander stood a bit straighter than usual as he went into his tree pose stretch. Talking softly, he and Merlin shared information and insights, while Xander went through his morning routine, but he froze in mid-stretch when Merlin said, "I never told Purr about my suspicions about Jingle-bells, but I figure he has some, too."

Instead of entering twisted triangle, Xander sat down with a thump. "Why do you say that?"

"The way he greeted her at the benefit."

"I wasn't close enough to hear them." But he'd watched them from behind the big potted plant and he hadn't observed anything different from the way Lord Purrmetheus greeted anyone else. Of course, he hadn't expected the greeting to be quite as forceful, as it had proven to be, when he'd experienced it for himself.

"It wasn't what he said." Merlin said. "It was the physical greeting. When he gave her cheek rubs, I don't think he actually touched her.... I can't be certain, but from where I was, they looked more like the air kisses some humans greet each other with. However, I know that the head butt was a token gesture."

Great Hathor, the head butt he'd experienced would have landed him on his tail, if he hadn't been so well trained. Thankfully, he'd been a bit more gentle with Mischief, but she had been put off balance, though he didn't recall Sari needing to sidestep during hers. "So you're saying he wasn't really happy to see her and he doesn't trust her," Xander concluded, since cheek rubs conveyed how much a furiend had been missed and head butts showed trust. He rubbed his shoulder where Lord Purr had connected and realized that the old tom had total confidence in him, Mischief, Killmouskie, Catula and Merlin. Purrhaps there was more to that unusual greeting than he'd first though. For certain, from now on, he would watch the old Purrtector to see exactly how much energy he put into greeting others.

Merlin made the sound of agreement. "Hey Pal, can I ask you a question?"

"You just did," Xander said with a laugh.

"Do you think we'll be able to wrap this Moreau mess up in the time we allotted?"

"I sincerely hope so."

"Me, too." Merlin sighed. "This grind of marketing and dealing with issues in my Purrtectorate is exhausting and I'm not getting any younger.... Pal, I'm thinking about stepping down and letting a younger cat pick up the load."

Xander blinked rapidly, as the real meaning sank in. "And I've spent months adding to your burden by asking you to help me investigate this mess. I'm so sorry and if you -"

"You never asked me, I volunteered and don't you dare think you're going to cut me out on this. What we're doing is important.... Letting everyone know how healthy pumpkins are pays well, but it isn't meaningful."

Xander blinked, again. "Are you saying you're tired of being the spokescat for Elegant Eats?"

"Of course!... What did you think I was talking about?"

He scratched his ear. "That helping me was making you too busy and I haven't asked you for help with just the investigation, there's Tadpole's surfing lessons, too... Do not feel obligated to do that and -"

"Hold up!" Merlin shouted, effectively cutting him off, again. "That is something I've been looking forward to for months, so do NOT tell me that I'm too busy to ride a few waves with her."

Xander didn't realize he'd been holding his breath until it whooshed out. "It's the same with her." He shook his head. "Both of you would make much better Sea Purrtectors than I do."

"Rubbish!"

"No, it's not. It's true. While I can surf, parasail and swim with some proficiency – thanks to your lessons – I don't love water like you and Mischief. You should have become the Sea Purrtector, instead of me and I suspect that when the time comes, Mischief will be much better at the job than I've ever been... A lot of times, I've wished you'd been appointed instead of me, because you're so much better suited for this particular Purrtectorate. As is, when I get into a dicey situation, I usually get out by asking myself what you would do."

"You seriously wish I'd been appointed in your place?" Merlin sounded shocked.

"Absolutely!"

"But you love your job." Now confusion seeped into his tone.

"I love serving Catamondo and making life better for those in my Purrtectorate, but I'd trade Purrtectorates with you in a heartbeat."

There was a long pause before Merlin said, "So you wouldn't be upset if I was appointed a Sea Purrtector and you were given a different posting?"

"Of course not." Xander's tail swished. "In fact, I'd love that, but it won't happen."

"Why not?"

"The Council made this position for me and as long as I blunder along without totally messing up, everything will continue on a more or less smooth sail... You know how they dislike rocking boats." He hoped his pal appreciated the puns.

"You never know what the future will bring," Merlin said in a very odd voice. What did his pal know? Did he seriously want a Sea Purrtectorate instead of his own Western North American Purrtectorate? Xander wished he could trade, then they'd both be happier, but that was impossible. He needed to believe that he was where he was supposed to be, doing what he needed to do and making the world a better place, but sometimes it didn't feel quite right.

Sounds of movement came from the dining room. A peak around the door confirmed that Killmouskie had begun his morning routine and the others were waking. Xander and Merlin finished discussing the case and agreed to post updates to their cloud, where Fluffy could also access the information. After they signed off, each of them began working through his to do list.

=^.^=

While Countess Mundalar's route was direct, it was taking them through the worst slum Xander had ever seen – or smelled. Though he didn't want to believe it, his nose was telling him that the small stream flowing next to the narrow walkway was actually an open sewer. Didn't the local cats know how unhealthy that was? Couldn't they get their staffs to work together to bury pipes? And where did they get their drinking water?

Since his escort didn't give any evidence of noticing the situation, he didn't mention it or offer suggestions for improvement.

Walking fast and trying not to breathe, he noticed several small, scraggly humans turn their attention on him. Hadn't they ever seen a Siamese before? Paying more attention to them, he realized their focus seemed to be on his throat. His muscles went to full alert, when he calculated how much money they probably thought they could get for his sapphire-encrusted gold collar. The Countess moved closer to him, so apparently she'd noticed the threat, too.

It was nice of her to try and purrtect him.

Unfortunately, her lithe stripped body was blocking his ability to defend himself properly. Xander cleared his throat. "If you could move a bit to my right..."

"No."

"Excuse me?" he said, his attention on the raggedy, smelly humans.

"Those children are under the purrtection of Chairman Rowdy Meow."

What difference did that make? To the best of his knowledge the chairman lived in China, so even if they were under his purrtection, that did not mean he was here to purrtect others from them. "They're staring at my collar." And if they could sell it, they could probably get enough human dollars to feed and clothe them for the rest of their greedy little lives.

"Of course they're staring at your collar. It's a

magnificent piece of engineering and technology – very good looking, too." She smiled at him, which succeeded in making her fangs look even more menacing.

Xander swallowed. "Just how dangerous are they?" He peaked over he shoulder to get a better look at the ragamuffins.

Her smile widened.

His stomach twisted.

"Rowdy is a good tom," she said. Xander searched the shadows looking for the elusive tom, but only saw more grimy little human faces – all of which were watching him. "He oversees this orphanage and I help him as much as possible. It is our belief that if we begin with children, raise them with love and provide a good education as well as healthy diet, we are taking a step toward a better future for humanity."

It suddenly occurred to him that she hadn't moved close to purrtect him, she'd been purrtecting the urchins.

Countess Catula wasn't the first cat who had expressed the belief that humans could be redeemed and he was certain she wouldn't be the last. Many felines believed that the goddess Hathor had put humans on the Earth, not only to serve cats, but also to be caretakers for this world and its resources, which meant that in their own two-legged way, they were Purrtectors, too. His line of thought ended when the Countess stopped. He came to an instant halt, senses alert for whatever danger Catula had picked up on, but the only thing he saw was an elderly black tom with distinctive tuxedo markings moving toward them as if his bones were iron and his joints were rusted in place.

Abruptly, Countess Catula bowed low before the old tom. He didn't pause to question why Nashik's Purrtector felt it necessary to show such respect or worry about his own vulnerability; Xander bowed low, too. The old tom shuffled a couple steps closer, then sat down. Xander's nose twitched at its proximity to the dirt, but his extensive training allowed him to avoid sneezing. Countess Catula wasn't so lucky.

"Do you expect me to converse with the back of your heads?" a gravely voice asked.

Xander stood up, then realized he probably seemed intimidating, so he sat down and studied the old fellow. Up close, he looked oddly familiar and while he had the strongest sense that he knew the elderly tuxedo cat, he was equally convinced that he'd never met him... Actually, he didn't think he'd ever met a cat that looked that old, so either he was a young tom, who'd suffered horribly in life – which was easy to imagine, since he already felt years older after walking in this smelly area – or he really had lived for centuries.

"Master Mahat, you honor us with your presence," Countess Catula said, still dipping her head low. Did she do that out of respect or to hide her impressive fangs?

"Countess Mundalar, why would I not purrsonally thank such a gracious benefactor?" The gravely voice matched the face and arthritic body and why did the name Mahat sound so familiar?

Catula waved a dismissive paw. "Purrtector

Merlin Frazer provided the cases of food, I merely gave him your address."

"Well the orphans appreciate it and it will certainly make our Christmas dinner special."

"I shall let him know how much you appreciate it."

Xander glanced from Catula to Mahat and back again. Had he ever heard such a stilted conversation? And why was Countess Mundalar treating this old tom with even more respect than she'd given Lord Purrmetheus? Furthermore, how much longer did they need to stay in this stinking slum with its open sewer and buzzing flies?

Mahat's faded eyes turned toward him. "I object to violence because even when it appears to do good, the good is only temporary while the evil violence does is permanent." Xander nodded in agreement. Mahat blinked in surprise. "I'm amazed that the one who murdered that chupacabra would readily agree."

"Things aren't always as they appear," Xander said, then looking the old tom straight in the eye, he added, "It isn't wise to be overly sure of one's information, even if it came from a video on *The Daily Mews,* which didn't give all the details." Since he felt as if he was in a strong position, it was politically correct to appear weaker to the elder. "It is healthy to be reminded that the strongest might weaken and the wisest might err."

"Wise words for one so young," Master Mahat said. "So why did my great-granddaughter bring you here?"

"Actually, we were heading over to the old

Moreau factory," Catula said.

Mahat's nose wrinkled. "Nasty place. One of the worst polluters."

"But it's much cleaner, now." Catula turned to him. "The Godavari River had been dying due to pollution from the factories on its banks. My predecessor was responsible for most of the clean up, so I merely need to make sure there is no back sliding."

Having met the Moreaus, Xander was not surprised to learn they had disrespected the environment and left a mess for others to clean up. Much as he liked the fact that Catula clearly adored her great-grandfather, he didn't want to spend any more time in this fly infested place than he absolutely needed to. "I hate to rush you, but we really need to get to the factory to see if there might be any clues left there."

Master Mahat's ears perked up. "What sort of clues are you looking for?"

"It's rather complicated, but for one thing, Sari alerted me that symptoms suspiciously similar to bird flu I dealt with in The Dominican Republic have broken out in this area, plus according to some research a colleague did, there could be a couple of those DNA freaks the Moreaus created around here."

Mahat's expression became contemplative. "They did leave awfully quickly and if memory serves, there were rumors about some very suspicious experiments done there."

Xander leaned a bit closer to the old tom. "Do you recall any rumors about cats or anything else being left behind?"

Mahat closed his eyes and worried his lower lip in concentration, then the elderly tuxedo cat nodded. "Since the ones who'd been left behind were adults, I didn't accept them here, but as I recall, there were two."

"Ganas and Gandharvas?" Xander asked.

Mahat shrugged. "I never heard any names, just a description, which seemed preposterous." He snorted.

"How come I've never heard about them?" Catula asked.

"My dear one, this happened when you were merely a twinkle in your sainted mother's eye."

Say what? Xander blinked in confusion, then realized the old tom meant that this had happened before Catula had been born. "Do you recall their descriptions?"

Mahat snorted, again. "Indeed I do, but there were not descriptions." He emphasized the S. "They were supposedly identical twins... Purrhaps abominable snowman would be more of a correct way to describe them. Of course, the abominable snowman is traditionally represented as being white as snow, while that pair was consistently described as being shades of gray."

Xander glanced around. There was a thin layer of grayish dust everywhere, so it wouldn't surprise him if this area ever got cold enough to snow, it would be gray instead of white.

A fat drop of rain splatted onto the grimy ground

and burst into a myriad of tiny droplets. "Afternoon rains are here," Master Mahat said. "Come inside while Hathor cleans our world."

Despite the oddly worded offer, Xander was quick to follow the elderly tom. His title might be Sea Purrtector, but there was nowhere in his job description that said he needed to get wet doing it and unlike Mischief, he did not look for opportunities to get soggy. Prior to ducking under the stained gray cloth that served as a door, he glanced in the direction of the market which was where Lady Violet and Killmouskie had taken Mischief. The clouds were darker there. As thunder boomed making his fur hover, he hoped his willful apprentice was not dancing in the rain and making everyone question her sanity.

Unfortunately, he knew she would stay true to her character and there was a good chance she already looked like a drowned calico rat.

With a sigh, he ducked under the shabby fabric, expecting more squalor, but was pleasantly surprised to discover a clean, tidy residence, which was illuminated with light from a window high on the wall. Individual cat cubbies were stacked from floor to ceiling. Better yet, the subtle scent of pine somehow overpowered the open sewer and stench of the ghetto. How had Master Mahat managed to achieve this place of peace and tranquility in such a dreadful area?

"Kaberi, are you here?" Mahat called.

"Yes," came a distant meow. As they settled on soft cushions in the comfortable salon, a chubby, sweet-faced black cat waddled into the room.

"Welcome!" Her glance moved past the rain-washed window then settled on Catula. "Did you come to help with the pre-holiday cleaning?"

"No, but I'll be back to help with that in a couple days," Catula said, with no hint of negativity that the older one might expect someone with the rank of Purrtector to be above lending a paw with manual chores. Xander's opinion of Catula inched upward.

"I know you!" Kaberi's dark gaze no longer looked completely welcoming. "Why are you with my niece?"

As Xander explained his interest in Chester Moreau and the evil experiments, which had apparently begun in the old factory, several kittens entered the room. The youngest was so young that it looked like her eyes had only been open for a few days, while the oldest looked as if his first birthday would soon be here. Yet one and all showed Kaberi, Master Mahat and Countess Catula the utmost respect. Whatever they were doing here, aside from keeping their residence clean and sweet-smelling, they were obviously doing an excellent job instilling good values in the next generation.

By the time the rain ended, Xander had learned a great deal about the way the Moreau chemical factory had contributed to the pollution problems of the Godavari River, the earth its waters touched and the air that its vapors blended with. He shivered over the way Mahat's description of the creeping devastation reminded him of a horror movie his staff had had the poor taste to watch. But what really bothered him was that he couldn't recall how the movie's hero had managed to overcome the creeping cloud of death.

Kaberi's chubby jowls jiggled as she reminded Mahat that most of the Godavari River had recovered so well that humans now were often seen swimming there.

Xander recalled that the market was near the river. He hoped Mischief didn't jump in for a paddle and could only imagine Lady Violet's horror, if his apprentice behaved around her, as she did with him.

Eventually, Mahat's wandering monologue turned back to the 'abominations' he'd originally mentioned. Fortunately, instead of simply referring to them as being shades of gray, this time he described them as, "Those two were the weirdest things I ever did hear of. Truffles said that they looked like short-hair black cats, who were wearing the long-fur gray pelts of their enemy and that wasn't far off from what they looked like."

Kaberi tilted her head to one side. "I think I might have heard of them, too, but I never actually saw them." She shuffled her paws. "And until now, I thought they were just some imaginary thing, like the invisible best furiend so many kittens have."

By now, Xander was completely curious about what the pretty little plump matron knew. "So, what were you told?" he asked.

She giggled with embarrassment. "What I was told, could not have been true. Can I interest you in a dried salmon treat? Sponsors of our orphanage are purrticularly generous during the holiday season."

Dried salmon was Mischief's favorite food, but he purrferred bird. Would it be a breech of etiquette if he turned her down? Obviously their resources were limited and, assuming Merlin was already familiar with this sort of situation, he understood why Merlin was so intent on gifting the kibble kitchens with his gourmet food.

Catula spoke up, "I would love a salmon treat and I'm sure Mr. Xander would, too, though I suspect he is being too polite to say so."

Kaberi's dark face broke into a big smile, which displayed impressive fangs. Was she also a relative of Catula or did Catula call Master Mahat great-grandfather as a sign of friendship and respect?

Did it matter?

Probably not. What mattered was that Catula was showing him how to behave and Kaberi was a potential source of information, even though she obviously didn't think what she'd heard was believable.... Most of what he'd discovered about Chester Moreau was unbelievable, so the fact that she didn't credit her information as fact actually made him suspect whatever she'd heard was based on truth.

When she returned, she had enough treats for everyone, including the youngest, who raised her paw to bat it, then stopped halfway to the chunk as she noticed the others were nibbling theirs. Putting her paw down, she gave the pinkish lump a delicate sniff, then she nibbled a corner. Soon, she plopped down and holding the chunk with her front paws, began chewing on it with a vengeance.

"I had no idea you were so fascinated by kittens," Master Mahat said.

Xander realized he was staring at the young one and blinked. "She reminds me of someone, but I can't quite put my paw on who." He shook his head to clear his thoughts. "Would it be possible for me to speak to Truffles?"

"Why would you need to speak with her?"

"To see if she recalled anything about that pair. From the way you quoted her description of them, I assumed she was very observant and creative."

Mahat nodded in agreement. "You're correct about her. She was both of those things. Alas, she is no longer with us."

"I'm sorry to hear that," Xander said, genuinely compassionate for his obvious loss.

"Oh! No! I didn't mean to suggest that she'd passed on. Oh, no, no, no, no, NO! Indeed not. She has merely moved away from here and is now working as a mouser on a container ship. I am happy to provide you with her access code, if you don't mind email." The elder tom sighed. "I have no idea where in the world she might be."

Xander nodded in understanding. "Wherever she is, she's most likely in my Purrtectorate."

"I hadn't thought of that, but you're correct, again."

"If there isn't anything else you recall about that pair, purrhaps now that Kaberi is done passing out snacks, she'll tell us what she heard."

Despite the lady's protest, she eventually admitted, "I was told they almost walked like monkeys, which is ridiculous, since no self respecting cat would move that way." After he made sounds of encouragement, she added, "And that description of Truffles' was pretty close, too. I was told they had short black fur on their faces and legs, but long matted gray fur everywhere else. Initially, when I heard that, I assumed that some foolish two-leg must have sewn up some sort of costume for them or something."

Master Mahat nodded, "I had a brief glimpse of them, but I was about a block away, so their long grey fur might have been an outfit they put on, but I had the impression that it was their natural fur and at the time, I recall wondering if the fur on their legs and face had been trimmed."

"Why would anyone do that?" Catula asked.

"Well, as Kaberi said, their fur was quite matted – almost like the photos of dread-locks I've seen. So it must have been difficult to groom, plus fur that long would be miserably hot in this climate.... Yes, I can see why they would be motivated to have it cut off."

"But why not cut it all?" Kaberi asked. "Why just the faces and legs?"

That was also what Xander wanted to know, too. Assuming that he now had a clue what Ganas and Gandharvas looked like... and if Kaberi was correct about what they walked like, were this pair of misfits a product of monkey DNA mixed in with cat? If they had, what might that mean? Would they have handy-dandy opposable thumbs, that could open cans of delectable delights? Would they have the strength of a gorilla? The ability to use their tails to swing through trees?

Xander inhaled so sharply that a bit of dried salmon got stuck in his windpipe. He coughed. Then coughed some more. Soon, his eyes began to water. Catula slapped his back so hard that he spat out the sliver of now strangely slimy fish. "Thank you!" he gasped.

Eyes were huge with worry, she asked, "Are you all right?"

He nodded. When he could speak, he said, "I shouldn't think and swallow at the same time."

Her eyes narrowed as she looked him up and down. "You're sure your all right?"

"Absolutely." He looked around, noticing that almost all eyes were on him and they look worried, so he explained what he'd been thinking about. Though they all still looked apprehensive, they were no longer looking at him as if he was about to leap over the Rainbow Bridge, but one skinny young tom's eyes were fixed on his mostly uneaten chunk of freeze-dried salmon. Xander focused on Kaberi and asked her if she knew of anyone else who might have seen the creatures.

"You think there is any possibility they could be real?" Her shock was tangible.

"Did you see the video clip of the ones called Vi-Purrs?" She nodded. He raised a brow.

Her golden eyes seemed to double in size. "That thing was real, not some photoshop creature?"

He nodded.

"Oh! Well!" She blinked rapidly, then gave him the name of a cat who had given her the description and then, she mentioned that she knew the cat who owned the person who had been the janitor for the factory. "She's pretty old, now, but I'm certain her memory is still sharp. I'll call her and ask her what she might remember." With that, she bustled out of the room and Xander used the opportunity to flick the unwanted chunk of salmon to the thin tom, who gulped it down quicker than a blink.

As soon as the rain ended, Xander followed Catula to the factory. The Nashik Purrtector's style rose in Xander's opinion when she used a laundry line as a tightrope to avoid getting wet. Thank Hathor he'd chosen such a creative, agile cat as a guide!

Once they got to dry pavement, they were able to walk side by side. They discussed the information Kaberi and Master Mahat had provided and Catula admitted, "I can't figure out how you knew I had this problem in my Purrtectorate, when I didn't see it."

"You're kept busy with the problems and apparently actually know many of the cats in your Purrtectorate by name." She nodded in agreement. "Have you ever met Chester Moreau?"

Catula shook her head. "The Moreaus left the country before I was born. Until the articles in *The Daily Mews* the only thing I knew about Moreaus was that it was the name of the factory that was the worst polluter of the Godavari River, but by the time I was voted Purrtector, even those waters were clean."

"So they're more like a legend or something."

Her face scrunched in thought, then she slowly nodded. "I hadn't realized it, before, but yes, you're right." She looked up at the narrow strip clouds, which were visible above the alley. After a long moment, when his jaw threatened to twitch from clamping tight, Catula's posture relaxed and he knew she'd made a decision.

But what had she been thinking about?

# Chapter 8

X ander expertly flicked the claw he'd inserted in the dusty lock and the tumbler rolled into place, a fraction of a second later, the padlock fell open. He tossed it aside, then positioned himself to provide proper leverage. The squeal of long-rusted hinges hurt his ears and the awful stench of mildew boiled from the shadowed interior made it impossible to breathe, but he continued to apply force until he and Catula could fit through the gap.

Once inside, Xander and Catula stood shoulder to shoulder and stared at the dusty stacks of boxes. "Where do we begin?" she asked.

He studied the labels, then pointed to a box the third layer down of nine and the forth in the row of ten. "That one." Without waiting for her to ask why, He leaped to the top of the stack, sank his front claws into the cardboard, which proved to be stronger than it looked, then with a violent sneeze that he couldn't control, he slammed his rear paws against the lower box and pulled with his front.

The box moved an inch.

He repeated the movement three times. Finally, the box flipped out of the space and plummeted toward the door. With a resounding bang and a cloud of dust, the door burst all the way open.

Xander did a flip, then gracefully landed on top of the battered box. "That's one."

The second box was easier to move, because his weight on the front counterbalanced it. Without the ceiling's impediment, it flipped down on his first kick. It landed on top of the first one.

Despite the shorter distance, he landed on top.

Catula's amber gaze was fixed on him. "I've never seen anything that amazing," she whispurred.

Xander blinked in surprise. "Don't you have kickboxing tournaments here?"

"Of course we do, but I have never, ever seen anyone move like that."

"Don't give me any compliments, yet. The next one is the trickiest."

"But why, when the second one looked easier?"

Xander stretched up, sank his front claws into the musty cardboard and gave a tug. "Because, this is the one I want to look through, so I need it to land in a convenient place." He glanced over his shoulder at her. "You might want to move to one side... I intend this to land just outside this room, where the light is better."

Before he'd finished his sentence, she'd jumped out of the way.

Another tug moved it forward far enough for him to wedge in behind it, but not enough so it would tip on its own. With a well-planned leap, Xander got behind the box, then kicked it. The box sailed over the other two, through the door and landed under the hallway's light.

Catula cheered, as if he'd just won a kickboxing match. Obviously, his years on the circuit had honed skills that were useful, even when there wasn't a Vi-Purr trying to kill him.

Hopping down, he extended his index claw, expertly cut the tape holding the cover on, then popped it off.

"You're amazing," Catula purred.

"Thanks. Now let's see what's in here." Xander clicked on his collar's recording feature.

"How come you chose this box?"

He raised a brow. "Which one would you have chosen?"

She bit her lip, nearly puncturing it with one fang, as she studied the dingy labels. "The one that says 'records'."

"Well, if we don't find what we're looking for in here, we'll check that one next." He pulled out several scraps of paper and scanned them front and back, then repeated the process several times, until he noticed Family: Cercopithecidae; Genus: Macaca listed under comments about the Western Ghats

Mountains. If his education served him – and he was confident it did, Cercopithecidae were monkeys. And if Kaberi's description was correct, this could provide proof for his theory about Chester mixing monkey and cat DNA. Xander carefully read the scratchy writing, then had his collar give him information on Macaca. He learned, 'The lion-tailed macaque has a black, shiny coat, except for a long, mane of grey hair framing the face and a long, thin naked lion-like tail with a tuft of black fur on the end. The genders are similar in appearance, although males are larger in size and have prominent canines.' He related the information to Catula.

"Seriously?" She leaned over to read the paper. "The Western Ghats Mountains aren't far from here, so how come I've never heard of those, before?"

"I don't know, but I think it's safe to speculate that if Gandharvas and Ganas were one of Chester's experiments, they could be part monkey and look like the abominations Master Mahat described."

Catula chewed her lip so hard that it began to bleed. "Until you got here, I thought I was doing a good job..." She got quiet, but her tension seemed to increase.

Xander gave her a gentle head butt. "Remember, this factory has been closed for years. When Merlin found the references for Gandharvas and Ganas, the names were associated with Mumbai, not here. If Chester moved away, there is every reason to think that any misfits he left behind would move, too." Thus, the better question was why Sari claimed that she'd never heard of the pair...

Side by side, he and Catula studied every scrap of paper in the box. By nightfall, Xander's fur was so filthy that the chocolate fur on his tail looked more like dark gray charcoal. As they made their way over the bridge, the temptation to leap into the river's tan colored water startled him.

Had he lived around Mischief too long?

Was he losing his purrspective on being a propurr cat?

Catula glanced at him, as if sensing his strange thoughts. Abruptly, she clamped her lips together and turned her attention forward. Unfortunately, her trembling stripes suggested that she was holding back laughter. "What's so funny?" he demanded.

Her loud yowl of laughter startled him. Once that was out, she laughed so hard she had to sit down, right there on the sidewalk in the middle of the bridge.

He sat next to her.

Humans dodged around them, as they hurried to wherever they were going. Xander took a deep breath – nearly sneezed – then overcoming the tickle in his nose, counted to ten. After he blew out his frustration, he calmly repeated his question.

"You – you – you h-have a c-cobweb st-stuck on t-top of your head." Catula laughed so hard her amber eyes watered.

He ran his paw between his ears. Sure enough, there was a clump of cobweb there. He wiped his paw on the concrete and kept his attention on her, as he tried to ignore the wisp of web that insisted on clinging to his paw.

Were wisps of cobweb still on his head, too? Catula's glances and subsequent laughter suggested that he hadn't gotten it all.

How long had that web been there?

Thank Hathor there wasn't an icky spider in it!

He scraped the sticky gunk off his paw, then felt the top of his head for stray strands. His skin crawled, as if a zillion bugs were sneaking around his sable pelt.

Dear Hathor, he needed a bath!

More people brushed past them. A human rode past on a bicycle with a large stalk of small green bananas tied to each handle bar.

"Okay, so I look silly and we're both filthy," he said. "We can either sit here and laugh or we can do something constructive." He stood up. "I'm sure I can find my own way back." He purrposefully headed toward shore and a certain jacuzzi he'd noticed near Castle Tower.

Catula quickly caught up with him. "I apologize for laughing. That was very wrong of me and I know better." She sighed. "It's just that you looked so – so – so"

"Ridiculous?"

Her mouth dropped open, then after a heartbeat, she nodded. "You looked so purrfessional, but then..." a fit of snickers cut off the rest of her thought.

"A bit of grime doesn't take away

professionalism." He squared his shoulders, then picked up the pace. The sooner he got to that tub and washed off the day's grime, the better. Soon, Catula was jogging after him, too intent upon keeping up to have breath for laughter or mindless chit-chat. When he came to the fenced patio surrounding the jacuzzi, he dodged through the metal bars and made a beeline to the clean water.

Something dove in right after him.

A peek told him that Catula had followed his example, so he held his breath and focused on scrubbing the mold, dirt and other nasties out of his fur. After a minute, he needed more air. One big gasp, then he re-submerged and resumed his cleaning efforts.

It took several minutes before he was satisfied with the results.

By the time he jumped out of the tub, Catula had dripped a large puddle onto the colorful pavers surrounding the tub. Xander respectfully moved away from her before he gave himself a through shake.

Was something wrong with him when damp felt better than dirty?

Catula seemed to shake herself out of whatever strange mood had preoccupied her and gave she herself a good shake. "Shall we finish grooming at my place?" she asked.

"After you." He gallantly tilted his ear.

"Good, it's more private." She quickly moved toward the fence.

He glanced upward at the tall wall of windows,

which overlooked the small courtyard, which the jacuzzi was in, then he looked at the water, which was considerably grayer than it had been. Had the strands of spiderweb floating on the surface come from his paw or head? Either way, he was finally rid of the disgusting thing... and hopefully its maker was long gone, too.

Upon entering her apartment, Xander heard a familiar yowl of indignation. "You are unbelievable!" Mischief growled. "You send me to the market to research those two abominations while you play around and have fun!"

Catula's head swiveled from his apprentice to him. "What makes her think that?"

"She loves playing in the water and we're obviously wet."

"Are you serious?"

"I'm afraid so."

Catula's shoulders started to shake and her fangs became more prominent as she tried to hold in her laughter.

Xander turned to face Mischief. "If you want to take a dip, just ride the elevator down to the ground floor, go to your left, then slip through the metal fence. You'll find a jacuzzi there."

"And?" Mischief demanded.

"And what?"

"Are you going to apologize for making me do all the work?" By now she was so close he could see green fire flashing in her glare.

"One, you didn't do all the work. Two, if you haven't had a bath, since you returned from the market, you had a much cleaner job. Three, when you go to jump into the jacuzzi, make sure you don't land on that cobweb – darn thing was hard as tar to get off."

Catula snickered. "And he looked ridiculous with it draped over the top of his head."

Mischief's glower faltered. "You took a bath because you had a cobweb stuck to you?"

"That and my tail looked more charcoal than chocolate."

"Actually, he looked like a black cat," Catula said.

"So you're wet because you needed a bath, not because you were having a spa day," Mischief said. "That figures. He never takes one unless there is no other alternative."

Catula cleared her throat. "Yes and no. Xander did the filthy parts, I just read and sorted old documents, so I didn't actually need a bath, like he did."

Mischief's green eyes narrowed. Fortunately, her look wasn't centered on him. "Explain."

Catula cleared her throat, again. Then she glanced around to make sure no other ears were close. "I'd been following his lead and didn't think when he ducked through the fence." Her nose turned red. "I didn't realize I'd leaped into the water until my belly hit and then it was too late."

"I wondered why you got out so quickly,"

Xander teased.

Mischief's mouth flattened. "So you're another of them that hates water."

"All cats hate water," Catula said.

Mischief shook her head. "Not all. For one example, I love water and for another, tigers love to swim.... you're a tiger cat, so I figured you'd know how to appreciate water, too."

"Sorry to disappoint," Catula said, though she didn't look the least bit sorry. "Listen, I need to... um, do some um.... stuff." She headed toward her bedroom. "Make my excuses and tell everyone what we learned." She ducked through a door and a moment later, it slammed shut.

Mischief looked from the hallway where Catula had gone to him. "You find anything interesting?"

He nodded.

"Good. I think we might have, too, but what we discovered seems to create more questions than answers." Her glance darted toward the living room where he could see Lord Purrmetheus tapping out a message on his iPhone. "How well do you think he knows Ms. Sari?"

"Can't tell, but Merlin doesn't think he's purrticularly fond of her."

Mischief took a threatening step closer to him. "You and Merlin talked about her and you didn't tell me? Is this some sort of double standard?" She growled low in her throat. "You tell me that I always need to tell you information, because you need to know and you even insisted that I learn to tell you by tapping it out, so I don't need to wait for a 'convenient time' and then you know something important like that and don't bother to tell me! Unbelievable!"

Xander leaned close and whispurred into her ear, "This morning, he told me he bugged her collar. I'm fairly sure Killmouskie understands code, so this is the first opportunity I've had to mention it to you. If we were still in her Purrtectorate, I would have found a way to let you know a.s.a.p. As is, she isn't around, so I felt we had the luxury of appearing casual."

"Well, I guess that's okay."

"What is?" Lady Violet asked.

Mischief visibly jumped, than looked so guilty about being caught gossiping that Xander said, "Someone was upset about my wet fur, so I explained that I'd been forced to take drastic measures."

"I hope it was worth it," the grand dame said.

He nodded. "I believe so and I'll tell everyone what Ms. Catula and I learned, when I only need to do so one time."

"Then come in here and start talking," Lord Purrmetheus ordered.

Xander was surprised that Lord Purr didn't push his iPhone aside. What was more important than clearing up the Moreau problems once and for all? Still, when Lord Purrmetheus motioned for him to speak, he began telling Mischief, Whiskers Killmouskie, as well as the Lord and his Lady what he and the Countess had learned from the old papers. He'd just gotten to how the papers suggested that Kaberi's information about Chester mixing monkey and cat DNA could be accurate and was describing Macaca monkeys appearance when an enraged human voice screamed, "Catula get back here!"

Xander stopped speaking as he swiveled to look where the shout had come from. Was his hostess in trouble for inviting them? Some staff could be very fussy about having strangers visit.

The sound of claws dashing over the tiled floor preceded her arrival. She put the brakes on to make the turn into the living room and nearly slid past the door, then got traction at the last moment, dashed in and dove under the sofa.

Again, the human called for Catula.

Not a breath came from under the sofa, but the sound of human feet was stomping closer.

Xander and Killmouskie looked at each other, wondering what to do. Then, without a syllable being said, the five of them ducked under the television armoire... if they were the source of Catula's present problem with staff, it wasn't wise to be obvious...

To his surprise, Lord Purr kept typing, despite being in hiding. Mischief gave the elderly Purrtector a long glance, then turned to him and tapped out, "W h a t i s w r o n g i n h i s P u r r t e c t o r a t e?"

Killmouskie looked at Mischief with surprise, then as the female human screamed at the sofa, ordering Catula to get out, he whispurred, "It's a Council problem."

Mischief blinked in surprise. "He's on the Council? Wow! I had no idea he was that important!"

"Didn't you study government?" Killmouskie

asked.

"Of course I did and I know exactly how Hathor set it up and all the changes that have been made since." She frowned. "I just never expected to meet anyone that important."

Killmouskie scratched his ear, but any comment he might have made was drowned out by the human shouting about how she needed to work from home and Catula had been told to keep her paws off her laptop. The human shook the offending machine as she glared at the sofa. "I know you're under there and I know what you did! In fact, I have proof!"

Catula's face poked out from under the sofa. The human tapped the USB stick that was plugged into the laptop. "Did you realize this clocks me in? It also takes a picture after three incorrect login attempts and you obviously tried to log in three times because my computer took this perfect picture." The human flipped the top up and for a brief moment the screen was turned toward the sofa; the photo of Catula's frustrated expression was priceless.... If the human was being honest about why it had been taken, it was also very incriminating.

The five of them watched with interest as Catula came out of hiding and began to calm her staff. Xander noticed that she never made any promises not to touch the laptop and by his calculations the only thing the ridiculous tantrum had accomplished was that he'd learned those odd bits stuck into a computer's USB could have a sinister purpose. He sent a photo of the thing to Fluffy and Merlin with a warning that if they ever saw one installed, they only had two tries to crack the computer's password before they could be busted – with evidence of their attempted break-in.

Within minutes, Merlin wrote back thanking him for the timely warning. He'd had one failed attempt at cracking Sari's computer code and certainly didn't want her to know she was under investigation.

Fluffy also responded, but said she'd never seen anything like that and wondered if the things were world-wide or mainly in India.

After Countess Catula calmed her staff, she directed her chef to prepare a lovely dinner. As they ate, Killmouskie, Lady Violet and Mischief related the events of their trip to the market and as Killmouskie shared some boring information on how to choose the best grapes, Xander understood why Lord Purrmetheus was ignoring the conversation in favor of whatever on-line chat he was engaged in. What wasn't as easy to understand was why he was barely eating the purrfectly purrpared chicken dinner and typing so furiously on his iPhone. What sort of problem was the Council dealing with?

He would have offered his assistance, but suspected that if he did, he would look like a snoopy catarazzi instead of a Purrtector who was genuinely concerned about the affairs and well-being of Catamondo.

As he chewed thoughtfully, his collar signaled that he'd received a communication from Sari. Xander swallowed then played it. "Today, my sources claim there have been a total of ninety-seven new cases of the illness you think could be bird flu. I need to purrtect my city and Maharashtra as a whole. Are you having any success finding the source of this?" He was glad he'd swallowed the delicious bite of chicken because he was certain he'd have spit it out, otherwise. How dare she act like the possible epidemic was his problem!

Mischief nudged him, then her claw tapped, w h a t i s w r o n g?

He tapped back that he didn't know exactly what was wrong, but Sari had reported new cases of the illness. Lord Purrmetheus had chewed his lower lip to the point of a drop of blood being visible and he wished there was a way to help him. Was he worried about the possibility of bird flu or was it something else? Because, if the flu was what was making him worry, then he was already doing his best to solve that issue. But, Xander doubted that the Council issue pertained to the flu because Lord Purr's only interest in their investigation had been to offer transportation and introductions to Countess Catula.

Mischief tapped out that if Lord Purr was a Council member, they were already helping him because they'd come here at the Council's directive to clear up any loose ends left by Chester Moreau. As she finished stating her opinion, Killmouskie laughed out loud. Mischief's head swerved toward him so fast that her fur looked like it was in a strong breeze. "Are you laughing at me?" she meowed.

"No..." Killmouskie admitted, "It's just that I didn't realize your generation still used the old code and I'd certainly never heard it tapped out with such emotion. Does my old heart good."

His apprentice watched Whiskers through

narrowed eyes, as if trying to determine if he spoke truth or not. "What do you mean by old?"

"It was used before there were phones."

Mischief blinked rapidly, as if it had never occurred to her that there had been a time when phones didn't exist and to give her credit, in her lifetime, they had always been readily available. And now that she had an apprentice Purrtector collar, she had access to all of Catamondo's public communications anywhere, any time. She blinked, again. "So you mean that everyone used to know the code, but now they don't bother to learn because of phones?"

"I'm sure there are many who still think it's important to learn, but most are too lazy." Killmouskie rubbed his ear. "Even before phones became the common form of communication, most were too lazy to learn the code, just like most were – and still are – too lazy to learn sign language." His smile revealed impressive fangs. "I didn't think about it at the time, but you're quite proficient in understanding that form of communication, too."

"Why do you ask, when you obviously know the answer?"

"It was rhetoric."

She blinked twice. Xander softly said, "Empty word that points out the obvious."

Abruptly Lord Purrmetheus batted his iPhone so hard that it skittered across the tile floor and only stopped when it hit the wall. Everyone stopped eating and talking to stare at him. Finally realizing he was the center of their attention, he sat down with a heavy sigh. "Mitzi insists that she will resign at the end of the year."

The room erupted in howls and yowls of surprise.

"But why?" Lady Violet asked. "She is very good at her job... who are you considering appointing until the next election?"

"Her assistant, Cheyenne, would be logical," Xander said. "She knows what is going on, so there would be less transition confusion."

"Hadn't though of that aspect," Lord Purr said.

"I've never purrsonally met her, but Merlin thinks highly of her."

Lord Purr scratched his ear. "Something to think about."

"May I ask why Lady Mitzi plans to resign?" Violet asked.

"Health issues."

"Oh," she said, "they must be very, very bad if she feels the need to do something so drastic instead of simply take a leave of absence... I know she's had problems with her kidneys in the past. Is that what's wrong?"

Lord Purrmetheus sadly shook his head. "Cancer, though she didn't say where it was, so it might be in the kidneys. She'll be going through chemical treatments, which means that her veterinarian will be giving her poison in the hope that it kills off the cancer before it kills her." He sighed. "She's doing the correct thing by resigning because even though she's good at her job, we can't expect her to put that above her own health."

They all nodded in agreement, but none of them returned to eating. Apparently he wasn't the only one that thought the chicken no longer tasted so purrfectly purrpared, but was he the only one who wondered if Chester Moreau had somehow infected Lady Mitzi after his plot to clone her failed?

Before long he discovered that Purrsident Mitzi Montgomery's health had been a worry for the Council for well over a year, but they'd never expected her condition to deteriorate to the point where she felt forced to resign, particularly now, when the worry of Chester's creation masquerading as natural cats loomed over them. Was a DNA test adequate to verify heritage? Would possible candidates be offended if they were required to give a sample and endure a lengthly interrogation to confirm that they weren't what humans called a 'deep cover mole'?

Lord Purrmetheus cleared his throat. "I am not really allowed to discuss Council business with anyone but them — at least not until we've arrived at a decision for how we want to handle the problem." He turned a solemn gaze on each and every one of them and lingered on Mischief. "With one exception, each of you is a well-known cat of prominence and you have either been a Purrtector in the past or you still are."

Mischief's nose turned bright pink as she stood up. "Are you asking me to leave because this is classified?" Her body language looked as if she was ready to make a dash for it.

Lady Violet wrapped her tail around Mischief. "He's telling you that he's trusting you not to mention this conversation to anyone outside of this room."

"Oh." Mischief continued to look uncertain until Lord Purrmetheus motioned for her to sit down.

"My dear mate and trusted furiend, Whiskers, are already aware that when Fraser told me he planned to launch his new line of vegetarian cat food here, I asked him to do me a tremendous favor." Lord Purr moved his head, as if his neck was sore. "To make a long story short, certain things about our Mumbai Purrtector have given me pause for several years and I'd hoped that Fraser could gain her confidence and help me determine if I was merely being an old fuddy-duddy," he gave Lady Violet a significant look, "or if there was actually something off about her."

"Well, I don't like her very much," Mischief said. "She's rude and she dresses flashy and what cat in their right mind wears that many bells?"

"Now, now-" Lady Violet began to say, but Whiskers Killmouskie loudly cut her off.

"Those are exactly the things that bother me about her! Good for you for noticing!"

Catula nodded in agreement. "I've never understood her obsession with bells."

"I had the impression that she wanted everyone's attention," Xander said. "It seemed to me like everything she did was geared to making everyone notice her."

"You mean the bells and glitter?" Mischief

asked.

"That's certainly part of it, but when we were at Merlin's benefit, did you notice how loud her voice was? Either she's hard of hearing, or she was making a cheap attempt to get everyone to look at her."

"Cheap is a good description of her," Mischief mumbled.

Catula snickered.

Before the girls could devolve into a wardrobe discussion, Xander asked, "Has Merlin discovered anything one way or the other?"

"Possibly. Possibly not... He was able to determine that she'd made a trip to Maharashtra in Konkan Division, yet when I spoke with Kistan, that area's Purrtector, she had no idea why Sari would have been there. In fact, she hadn't even known she was there."

"Could it have been a purrsonal issue?" Lady Violet asked.

"That's always a possibility," Lord Purr said.

"But it just doesn't feel right," Xander said. "I know exactly what you mean, something about her felt a bit 'off' to me, too."

"Do you have anything tangible to base your feeling on?"

Xander shook his head.

"In that case, I think it is wise for us to focus on something that we can sort out." Lord Purr wrapped his tail around his toes. "Ganas and Gandharvas are another questionable pair and if what my dear mate tells me about her inquiries at the market is fact instead of rumor, there is a good chance that the two you are interested in are Moreau misfits." He cleared his throat, then added, "They need to be tracked down and their intentions toward Catamondo must be determined... Very glad you are handling that."

They all nodded is agreement.

Xander wished finding them could be a simple and straightforward as India's chief Purrtector made it sound, but thus far, he didn't see any pattern to the unrelated bits of information they had gathered about Ganas and Gandharvas. Still, the more he learned about them and their possible origins, the more he was convinced that Merlin's suspicions about them were worth the miserable trip here.... air-pockets included.

# *Chapter 9*

**M**ischief batted a tiny knot of purple silk back and forth between her front paws, but her attention was on the moon reflecting off the rain-spotted sliding glass door, which led to Catula's narrow porch. Abruptly, she stilled the makeshift ball with a firm paw, turned her attention to him and said, "We have GOT to figure out a pattern to these clues and get this sorted out within the next couple days."

Two days to resolve the mess? They'd been looking for information and leads for months. "How do you expect us to do that?"

"I don't know, but I know Mr. Merlin will be finished with his marketing stuff in two days and if we have this sorted out by then, I can go surfing." Her eyes narrowed to slits, "But he's like you and too responsible to have any fun if there is a way he can improve things or help Catamondo's security." She hissed. "You and Mr. Merlin need to figure out that you need a balance of fun and work."

"For me, WORK IS FUN."

She blinked, obviously stunned by his uncharacteristic emotion. After a beat, she slowly shook her head. "That's what you say and purrhaps you even believe it, but I think you spent so many years on your strict schedule and diet that you've forgotten that it's okay to do something just for fun."

"I went to Merlin's benefit."

Mischief snorted. "That was work and you know it!"

Xander tried to think of the last time he'd done something spontaneous, but the only thing he could think of was making the decision to take Mischief on as his apprentice. Since then, practically every day, he wondered what had possessed him to do that. He cleared his throat, then asked, "Do you think the lead you had on Ganas and Gandharvas being seen at the Tansa Wildlife Sanctuary is a red herring or valid lead?"

"I can't be certain... Sahib was positive they lived at Moreau's old factory, but she also thinks that they moved to the Sanctuary, shortly after they got left behind." She scratched her ear. "Sahib said it was years and years ago and she hasn't heard any comments about them being in this area in a long, long time."

"Well, if you have confidence in her information, that's probably the direction they moved first, but if we're going to figure out where they went from there, I guess we'll need to consider going to Tansa."

Mischief threw the little purple ball of silk at him. "We should go directly to Jawahar Palace. I'm betting that's where they are now. I mean, four different cats brought up that location when we were chatting about misfits, strange events and stuff." Her tail thumped. "But I betch'a you ignore that for now because you always go from A to B to C and on and on, until you get to X, Y and Z, which is a total waste of our time. Worse, you're going to waste all Mr. Merlin's vacation time, too, by doing this in your tedious way, even though you can see that Jawahar is almost certainly where they are at.

"Jawahar Palace?" Catula said, as she passed by.

"Yes," Xander said. "Are you familiar with it?"

"Only that it's supposedly structurally good but it's also supposedly haunted, so no one actually lives there or takes care of it."

Mischief's whiskers bristled. "A neglected property is where I'd hide if I was a freak."

"From what I've heard, freaks live in places that actually look haunted, which is pretty common in some of our temples and old buildings. But, the outside of the palace looks majestic and historic. Its old stonework also makes it look sturdy...." Catula frowned. "Now that I think about it, what little I've seen of it is really in decent condition, so I wonder why no one lives there and they don't allow tour groups inside."

Mischief's glance darted back and forth between him and the countess before it settled on him. "You heard her. It's a grand old place and possibly livable, yet no one lives there and no one is allowed inside. AND if that isn't enough, it's supposedly haunted. NOW IF I was a Moreau freak, that is exactly the sort of place I'd choose to live AND I wouldn't want people calling me an abomination or freak or whatever, so I'd scare everyone away." She took two steps forward until their noses were touching. "You still think it's smart to follow your A to B to C pattern, or shall we save time and go directly to Jawahar Palace?"

He embedded his claws into the silly purple wad of silk so he couldn't smack her and tried to appear calm and relaxed about her insubordination. "What do we do if we can't find any trace of Ganas and Gandharvas there?"

"IF we can't find them or more recent evidence of where they are, then we go to the Tansa Wildlife Sanctuary."

"Which wouldn't be that far away from the palace," Catula said.

If Catula thought Mischief's plan was sensible, it would be stupid not to try it. "Fine. We do it your way." He flipped the purple rag ball back to Mischief, then tapped his collar to find out where the palace and wildlife sanctuary were located. Apparently both were near Thane, which was a city in the state of Maharashtra. But what really caught his attention was learning that Thane was in the Northern part of the Mumbai Metropolitan Region.

Was it a coincidence that Sari had made her mysterious trip in that direction?

The kid might be onto something solid... was

she correct when she claimed he wasted time making sure all pieces of information formed a solid pattern?

Could he trust her intuition or whatever she was basing her opinion on? He hoped so, because he planned to check out Jawahar Palace, tomorrow.

=^.^=

"I'm surprised that no one wanted to come with us," Mischief said, her attention on a herd of cattle that acted like they owned the road. The bus driver honked at the brazen cows and he revved the engine, but the closest cow merely flicked her ear at a fly.

Xander privately thought the walking hamburgers would be wise to show more respect to vehicles, which could break legs – or worse – but this was not his country and he had not come here to change any legislation. "Cattle are sacred, here."

She snorted. "It is wrong to have cows lounging on sidewalks and in streets like dogs!"

He didn't give into the temptation to nod. "Don't forget that as Purrtectors, we have to uphold our peace treaty with Dogdom."

She snorted, again. "This country is all messed up! No wonder that nut, Chester, created his freaks here."

Xander lowered his voice, "We are guests and should not criticize." He put his mouth to her ear and whispurred, "And you never know who might be listening."

Mischief gave him a mutinous look, then turned her glare to the lumbering cattle, who had no apparent respect for their bus. With the driver continually honking the horn, peace was impossible. Xander's thoughts were in a tumult, too. Was Mischief correct about going to the palace? While he could understand how Ganas and Gandharvas could easily have gotten downriver from the factory where they had been created; he couldn't quite make the mental leap from how they moved from the Godavari River, where the old Moreau factory was located, to the Tansa River, which was their destination. To the best of his knowledge, the Godavari and Tansa rivers never met. And for certain, he knew the Godavari traveled Southeast from Nashik to the Bay of Bengal, while the smaller Tansa River's main claim to fame was the lake at its origin, which had one of the largest masonry dams in the world. So, when his collar's monitoring program had detected that the bug Merlin had put on Sari was moving in their direction, he had thought it wise to expound on his interest in the Godavari River's potential as a way the two abominations had gotten away. Of course, Mischief had not understood that his comments to the others were designed to make them give Sari invalid information, if/when she arrived and asked where he was, so she was still radiating irritation and confusion. Better that, then outright declare that Sari could have risen to her rank under false pretenses. IF he found incontrovertible proof that she was guilty, that would be something else, but until he found that, there was always the possibility that she was simply annoying. Annoying purrsonalities were not his problem.

The bus jerked as it backed up, then moved forward, again, maneuvering about the tan bull that was lying in the middle of the lane. "Finally!" Mischief said, as the bus picked up speed. "That cow should be turned into barbecue!"

Xander scratched his ear. If she couldn't tell the difference between genders, was it his duty to instruct her? Was the gender of cattle relevant to completing his investigation? No!

The bus picked up more speed when it turned onto the wide interstate and headed Southwest. "I keep being afraid we're going to crash, but it seems like everyone here is backward," Mischief said, as two motorcycles zoomed around their bus.

Xander sighed. "Just because you've always lived in countries where they drive on the right doesn't mean it is the only way." He tilted an ear toward the driver. "Haven't you noticed that the steering wheel is on the right side instead of the left."

"But they don't DRIVE on the right. Traffic is on the left and that's just wrong."

"I guess it depends on how one looks at it, but if you think about it, whichever side the steering wheel is on, is the side where oncoming traffic comes from."

Her eyes narrowed. "Are you saying that whoever builds vehicles can't remember which side to put the steering wheel on?"

Was he? Xander blinked. "No, I'm just saying that there is more than one way to be right and fortunately we don't need to figure it out." His tail thumped the reddish fake leather seat. "Now, can we simply enjoy the scenery?"

"There isn't much to see except poverty and dust." She sneezed. "At least, I can tell Mama and Ms. Sharkey that Haiti and the Dominican Republic

Purrtectorates aren't the only ones with too many people, too much dust and stinky slums."

"Did you think poverty was confined to their Purrtectorates?"

She slowly nodded.

"Whatever gave you that impression?"

"Well, *The Daily Mews* for one thing... Haven't you noticed all the ads for gourmet kibble, luxury beds, high-tech toys and designer clothes?"

"Of course I have, but what does that have to do with anything?"

"Well, how about the articles they print about the lives of some cats – the photos of their penthouse, or beach cottage or from their vacations..."

"Are you telling me that you figure that cats all over the world live like royalty?"

"Are you suggesting they don't? I mean, look how Catula and the sorry one live and I know Merlin has a swank life."

"What I'm suggesting is that poverty is in all countries and there is no such place as Utopia, so each of us has to make the best of our purrsonal life."

"But the ads-"

"Purrpetuate a grand illusion designed for cats to beg their staff to buy them this, that and the other thing. Believe me, the photos only show the half of the story that they want you to believe." When it looked like she planned to argue, he raised a paw. "Think about Sari's apartment. Did it look like it could have been in one of the stories you're thinking of."

She eagerly nodded.

"Good, now think about the view from her balcony. Remember the slums?"

"Yes." Her tone was subdued.

"Now, how many cats within a kilometer of her home do you think live like she does and how many do you think live in poverty?"

"I think I understand what you mean about a grand illusion, she just has a nice place in the middle of stink, but most cats in her Purrtectorate probably have a hard life."

"Exactly!"

"Do you think Lord Purrs' problems are a big illusion, too?"

Xander sighed. "Unfortunately, no. I think he and The Council have a very big problem and I wish I could help them, but the best way we can do that is by doing the job they assigned us – making certain all the Moreau misfits and clones had been found, so that's what we'll do."

"It seems kinda silly since there hasn't been anything new since our encounter with the Vi-Purrs," she said.

"Can we be certain of that? What if cats in Sari's Purrtectorate are ill because of them? That is a possibility that we need to verify." For now, Merlin was keeping his eyes and ears tuned to information about more ill, any change in the status of those who were already ill and monitoring Sari's movements.

"Wouldn't it have been easier to stay in Mumbai and do that instead of go to Nashik?" Mischief frowned in confusion.

"Easier? Absolutely! Smarter? Doubtful."

"And you aren't going to tell me why, are you?"

Xander glanced around the bus, verifying that no one seemed to be paying attention to them. Then, he put his nose to her ear and explained that she had already been visibly antagonistic toward Sari, so it had been wise for them to leave Mumbai, as if there was nothing of interest there, which had given Sari a false sense of security and thinking that she was not under suspicion was forming a very interesting pattern.

Mischief scratched her ear. "You bugged her, didn't you?"

"I most certainly did not!"

She looked him up and down. He wrapped his chocolate tail around his toes. Mischief snorted. "Then someone else did, because you would not know about that 'interesting pattern' otherwise. So who did it? Lord Purr? Commander Killmouskie?... Don't tell me it was Lady Vi, because I was with her and I would have noticed."

Xander shook his head. "Sorry, but to the best of my knowledge they didn't do anything like that."

Her eyes narrowed. "But you are able to monitor her."

Xander shrugged.

She leaned close, which would have been a lot more threatening, if she'd been larger or had fangs like Catula. "How do you expect me to become a good Purrtector, if you don't explain what you're doing and why?... Mr. Merlin is keeping an eye on her, isn't he?"

"Yes. And he did bug her collar, but not at my request."

"Did he give you the tracking code?"

As he nodded, he raised his paw to send it to her collar. After all, she was right – how did he expect her to learn how to do the job if he left her in the dark? It wasn't as if she was still a silly baby, she was now his official apprentice. Her eyes widened when the connection was finished. "Satisfied?"

She didn't answer immediately and as she fiddled with her collar, her expression became more and more confused. "Are you sure you sent me the correct tracking code?"

He nodded and watched a truck carrying a camel pass their bus as he silently waited for her to figure it out.

"You're positive?"

Again, he nodded.

"Did you or Mr. Merlin bug any other collars?"

He shook his head.

"Do you think that my collar needs to have its GPS recatibrated?"

"No." He decided to give her a break, after all if he'd started monitoring Sari's movements at this point, instead of as soon as Merlin had given him the tracking code, he would have been confused, too.

"Her signal began moving North-north-east shortly after we got up and she arrived in Nashik about a half hour ago. That's why I was in such a rush to leave early and why I didn't tell anyone exactly where we were going or what our schedule was."

"You were afraid someone would tell her."

He nodded.

"But last night, Ms. Catula was there when we — you — decided that we would go directly to the Jawahar Palace."

He smiled. "True, but what was my main topic at breakfast?" He licked his lips, recalling the delicious shrimp bisque they'd been served.

"How the Godavari flowed to the Bengal Gulf... were you trying to make everyone think we were going in the opposite direction?"

Xander chuckled. "It seemed wise, since I didn't know if Sari might have managed to bug Catula's home or if any of them might say something I purrferred she didn't know. For instance, I adore Lady Violet, but she is quite chatty and even if she didn't intend to undermine my investigation, she might have said something, which Sari could figure out. And that is also why I was so pleased when Catula, who is the only one that knew our real plans, said that she planned to go help Master Mahat and Kaberi get everything ready for the holidays."

"You know you're purranoid, right?" The bus veered into the passing lane, then zoomed around a wooden cart piled high with onions, which was being pulled by two bulls with vicious looking horns. Though he was able to hold his position, Mischief almost slid off the seat. "Oh my whiskers!" She meowed, "Did you see that? Those are the first cows I've seen, since we arrived here that are doing something useful!"

He glanced back at the slow-moving bovines. Could they have been cows? Doubtful. Was she trying to distract him from her lack of preparedness for the bus to make an unexpected movement? He looked her up and down, evaluating her posture, hoping to detect why she seemed to have difficulty keeping her balance on car seats.

When he remained silent, her attention never wavered. In fact, the only clue about her state of mind was the way her claws had embedded into the fake leather seat. Finally, when she couldn't take it any longer, she demanded, "What did I say, this time?"

Say?

If that was what she wanted to believe he was focused on, fine. After all, it wasn't as if he'd figured out why she'd lost her balance – twice – while riding. Until he could figure out what she needed to change, he'd play it her way. "I think we need to focus some lessons on gender." He smiled to lessen the implied rebuke.

Whiskers stiff, her glare blazed with anger. "Did you just suggest that I am too stupid to know the difference between a cow and a bull?"

"Well, you did just call two bulls, cows."

"WELL THEN, maybe YOU need to take some of your own advice and research what you obviously do not know."

"My vision is excellent."

"This is about your vocabulary!"

"Excuse me?"

She took a deep breath as she visibly tried to calm herself, then she exhaled and said, "Cattle is the plural of cow, but cows is also proper and is commonly used colloquially for that type of large domesticated creature. They are a prominent modern member of the subfamily Bovinae, from which you get your word bovine... Cattle are raised as livestock for meat, as dairy animals and as we've just seen as draft animals. So, yes, it would have been more accurate if I'd said two bulls instead of use the colloquial cows, but I thought we were merely having a friendly chat and not some sort of gender test." Her tail continued to swish with anger after she finished speaking.

It was tempting to check the dictionary portion of his collar to verify her information, but he didn't need the distraction and she didn't need the insult, particularly when what she'd said sounded familiar. Instead, he focused on distant birds lazily circling upward in the air.

After several more silent minutes, Mischief growled, "Well? You have anything to say?"

He tilted his ears toward the distant vultures. "The shape of the wing is important in determining the flight capabilities. Did you know that a wing's shape tells how a bird flies?"

She shook her head.

"There are advantages and disadvantaged for

each type of wing."

"What do you mean?"

"Speed, energy use and maneuverability."

"Those look like the low energy type. Are they going in circles because of some sort of upward wind thingy?"

"I'm sure they are." Xander warmed to the topic, "The ratio of weight to wing surface is a big factor. Most bird wings are one of four types: elliptical wings, high speed wings, high aspect ratio wings and soaring wings with slots."

Mischief stared at the circling birds. "And those are?"

"Well, elliptical wings are short and rounded and best for tight maneuvering in confined spaces such as might be found in dense vegetation."

"So, they don't have those."

Xander smiled. "Correct. Hawks often have elliptical wings."

"And they probably aren't high speed wings, because they certainly aren't going up very fast."

"Correct, again. That type of wing is used by the bird with the fastest wing speed. Peregrine falcons and many ducks have them."

"So do those have the high aspect ratio wings?"

"That is possible, since that shape of wing is often used by gliding birds. The wing is longer than it is wide and is best for slow flight. We've seen several seabirds fly like that."

Mischief nodded, "So you're saying those birds have soaring wings with deep slots." Her forehead wrinkled. "How can you tell the difference, particularly at this distance?"

Xander laughed. "Their size is one clue. Soaring wings are common in larger inland birds, such as eagles and vultures."

Her gaze narrowed on the tiny forms. "Those are vultures, aren't they?"

He nodded.

She turned toward him. "What do having four types of wings have to do with our investigation?"

Xander shrugged. "Possibly nothing, but learning something new is always better than being bored. Besides, those vultures are demonstrating how to use updrafts."

"Ah, so you're back to that, again." She snorted. "If you ever get too old to be a Purrtector, you should become a Purrfessor."

"Interesting idea, but do you remember what an updraft is?"

"Of course I do! Its a small current of warm rising air that goes up until it reaches air that is the same temperature. Are there updrafts at Jawahar Palace?"

"I have no idea."

"About what? Updrafts or becoming a Purrfessor?"

"Updrafts form in various places, so there could be one at the Palace."

"And?"

"I'll consider it." There was no way he was going to deal with a classroom full of self-important kittens and try to get them to open their minds to learn. Not after his experience of taking on an apprentice! He was willing to live by Catamondo's Prime Directive and use his natural talents to make the earth and the life it supported better, but he was certain he did not have any natural teaching talent, so it would be a disservice to the teaching purrfession to even consider the idea.

She snorted, as if she could read his thoughts. "Sure you will."

Silence reigned for several miles. As the bus pulled into Atgaon's station, Xander got up. "Come on!"

"Why?"

"We're getting off."

"But we're only halfway to Thane!"

"Shhhhhh!" he hissed. "Don't draw attention to yourself!"

Mischief suddenly looked frightened. "What's wrong?" she whispurred.

"The same car has been following this bus for the past four stops." Hopefully, that was enough for her to understand that they needed to get off and see if the vehicle continued to follow the bus or if it stayed in Atgaon."

She deftly switched off her collar, which was something he'd done at the previous bus stop. Good, she understood the situation! Without being told,

Mischief shielded herself among the confusion of humans who were simultaneously getting on and off the bus. Best of all, she didn't need to be told that the driver's attention was the most important to be avoided; after all, he was the one who might be asked about passengers.

Once on the ground, Mischief darted behind a haphazard pile of bags and boxes. By the time he dashed around them, she had vanished. Xander hunkered down behind a lumpy bag, then peaked at the car, which was parked in front of a small restaurant about a half block away. Its beige color was similar to Sari's vehicle, but this sedan was older and its windows were mirrors, which reflected the sky. As a group of humans passed it, they gave the impression of walking on clouds, which was bizarre. When all the passengers had gotten off the bus, the driver jogged to the restaurant. As he vanished inside, the sedan's window opened a couple inches to reveal a matt-black interior. Xander's ears picked up a whistle and it only took a moment to spot a medium-sized dog get up and amble to the vehicle.

Due to music blaring from a kiosk selling bangles and baubles, his acute hearing couldn't pick up what was being said, but the brown dog's body language indicated it was negotiating and that theory was confirmed when something was dropped out the window. He thought it might have been a biscuit, but the dog gulped it too quickly for that to be confirmed. The overpowering scent of onions, from the lumpy white bag, not only made smelling anything else impossible, but his eyes were watering, which made things appear to swim. Now that payment had been received, the dog trotted to the bus and hopped aboard. Xander hoped there were enough conflicting scents that it couldn't track them, but he couldn't be certain. As a noisy group of children chattered their way between him and the car, Xander dashed to a kiosk displaying colorful fabrics and beaded jewelry. He ducked behind a bright yellow box and came nose to nose with Mischief.

"About time you got here." She leaned closer to him, sniffed, than gave a big sneeze, but didn't say anything about any clinging stench of onions or question his ability to see through his tears.

"I was trying to determine who was driving the car and looking for a license plate or something to identify it."

"Except for the windows, it's about as common as they come." Good, she'd noticed that, too! "So, the question is, how come they don't want anyone to see who is driving."

He blinked. "Why do you assume that's the reason for the windows?"

"A driver is always necessary, but passengers aren't and if they were hauling something a van or a truck would probably be the better choice."

"Good points. So, do you have any idea who might be driving?"

"Someone associated with the Moreaus, who knows we're in India and wants to know what we're doing and what we know."

"Any other possibilities?" He raised a brow, but didn't look at her, as his attention was focused on the bus, watching to see what the dog would do next. He was so focused on the door that he was startled when the bus driver returned, carrying a brown paper bag and white paper cup. A moment after he got on the bus, he shouted something, put down his drink and moved fast toward the back of the bus, where they'd ridden. There was a short scuffle and a yelp, then the dog leaped down the steps and sprinted back to the car.

"You really think there is any other explanation for that car?"

"Just because we have a peace treaty with Dogdom, doesn't mean they stopped keeping track of Purrtectors. If one was driving, they wouldn't want humans to know how skilled they were, which could explain those windows."

"I hadn't thought of that." Mischief frowned. "So how would they know we were Purrtectors?"

"Beats me." The dog sprinted to the car, where it began yapping at whoever – or whatever – was inside the tan sedan. Obviously, he was sharing whatever he'd discovered. But what had he noticed? While collars could be turned off and physical shapes could be made more difficult to see, scents were very difficult to conceal.

Abruptly, the tan vehicle reversed onto the road, almost broadsiding a bicycle. As the rider shook his fist and shouted insults, the car sped away in the direction they'd come from. Mischief snickered. The dog stood stiff-legged glaring at the receding vehicle. Why was its body language so angry?

"I'll ask." Mischief said.

Dear Hathor, he'd spoken his thoughts aloud!

What was happening to his control? "And how do you propose to do that?"

"March right up and ask."

"And if there was a Dogdom spy in the car, who told him who to look for?" Xander raised a brow and let that sink in for a moment, before adding, "Then all our efforts of putting whoever has been following us off the track will have been a waste of time."

"If they were going to describe anyone, they'd describe you. Your seal-point coat, non-crooked tail and un-crossed sapphire blue eyes are distinctive. Meanwhile, I'm just a plain calico."

"With a distinctive hot pink collar."

Her eyes widened. "Oh!"

"So, what can we do to make you look like a local cat?"

Realizing it was a rhetorical question, she began rummaging in a box, moments later pulling out several scraps of ribbon, which looked like a vibrant rainbow in her clenched paw. "Help me wrap these around it."

"A bit gaudy, aren't they?"

"So? It's available, which means these are probably what the average cat wears. Besides, if any hot pink is visible, it'll look less obvious than it would against some blah color."

She had a valid point. Xander grabbed a purple strand and began securing it around her collar. Next, he added lime green, then chrome yellow, red, royal blue, hot pink and orange. By the time he was done, she looked funky, but rather good – at least for a girl.

He hoped he never got into a position where he needed to wear anything so undignified.

"Wish me luck!" With a swish of her tail, she sauntered in the direction of the restaurant's trash bin. Xander was so intent on watching her casual progress and planning on how to back her up, if that became necessary, that he was startled when the bus's engine revved and a black puff of exhaust appeared from its tailpipe. As it pulled onto the road, he resigned himself to either finding another way to get to Tansa or changing his plans.

Instead of going directly to the dog, whose attention was still on the car, even though it was now merely a tan spec, as it sped away, Mischief went to the trash can. As she put her paws on the rim and peered in, the dog noticed her. With a snarl that Xander could hear over the blaring radio, the dog went toward Mischief. Xander's muscles tensed as he prepared to run to her rescue.

To her credit, Mischief didn't panic. She calmly turned to meet the potential assault and cocked her head. The dog slid to a stop mere inches away from her, but instead of attack, he sat down. Xander could see Mischief's mouth moving, but couldn't hear what she was saying, but whatever it was, the dog's expression changed from anger to confusion, to – was that some sort of smile?

Xander blinked three times and shook his head, but when he looked, they were chatting like they were --- friends? His eyes narrowed as he watched them amble side by side back to the trash can, then sit down next to it and continue chatting.

After several minutes and a lot of chit-chat that he couldn't eavesdrop on because of the loud music from the kiosk where he was hiding, Mischief got up, bid the dog a friendly goodby and ambled away. Instead of coming directly to him, she walked past without giving him a glance, then went into a food kiosk. At least the pictures looked like food and that was where the dreadful sack of onions had gone. Were pav bhaji, bhel puri and misal pao types of Indian food? He raised his paw to research the strange names, then remembered why he'd turned off his collar.

Dropping his paw back to the ground, he was glad no one had seen his lapse.

"Vaji said he didn't know the guy in the car – had never met him or seen the vehicle before," Mischief said from behind him.

How had she managed to sneak up on him?

"So you're now on a first name basis?"

Mischief nodded. "He's actually a decent sort."

He raised a brow.

She scratched her ear. "The guy told him to look for you on the bus – actually, he described you as a stuck-up Siamese know-it-all, but if he knew about me, he didn't mention me to Vaji."

Did others see him that way? And if so, was that good or bad?... Did how they thought about him matter? Xander shook his head, as he realized it was quite a compliment if those who were enemies of Catamondo viewed him as smart.

Mischief frowned. "Why did you shake your

head? That is exactly what Vaji told me."

"Sorry, I was wondering why we were being followed."

"Vaji didn't know, but he said whoever it was smelled weird and he was positive he wasn't a dog – no dog would make a deal for treats, then not pay."

"Did he say anything definitive about the scent?" What would a DNA misfit that was part monkey, part cat smell like?

Mischief cocked her head. "Yes, he said some trekkers smelled like that when they came back from Mahuli Fort."

His paws itched to consult his collar and learn more about the place, but he didn't dare turn it on, so he clenched his paws. Mischief's posture straightened, then she looked from his paws to his collar. "Do you really think they bugged you?"

"I don't know," he said, "but since we just got confirmation that someone was following us, I don't want to chance it."

She worried her lower lip. "Do you think mine could be compromised?"

"It's a possibility, but less likely, since, as an apprentice they probably don't consider you to be a viable threat." When her whiskers stiffened, he hastened to add, "What our enemies don't know is an advantage to us."

"Do you think it would be okay for me to turn mine on long enough to check where Mahuli Fort is, or do you just want to continue on our original plan?"

"That would depend where the fort is. If it's in

the vicinity, it would probably be wise to at least eliminate it as a possible hideout." He looked up the road, making certain the tan car wasn't in sight. "Just be quick about it and while you've got it on, drop Merlin and Fluffy a quick note telling them not to be worried about us being offline."

"Gotcha!" Her paw tapped the code into her collar, then her little calico face took on a look of intense concentration as she entered the mental link. Xander kept his attention on the road, ready to warn her at the first glimpse of mirrored windows.

# Chapter 10

*D*ear Hathor, what had possessed him to think accepting a ride on a camel was a good way to get to the fort? The beast lurched left-right, left-right as its long legs moved over the uneven trail.

"I thought you said I'd get used to the way this thing moved," Mischief meowed.

"That's what I heard." Obviously, Killmouskie had never ridden one of the dreadful things. Boat of the desert, indeed! And what were the things doing in India? Were there deserts nearby that he didn't know about? His paws itched to turn his collar on and research the issue...or maybe they simply itched because the beast's straw-like hair scraped his paws with every lurching step.

"Relax," Mischief muttered. "You don't need to do it just for your peace of mind, loosening your muscles and taking a deep breath will also calm the animal down and make the ride smoother." She snorted. "Who gave you that information?"

"I overheard Killmouskie and Lord Purrmetheus chatting while you were sleeping on the train."

"I bet it was all just hot air and they've never even been near one!"

He suspected she could be correct, but other things they'd said seemed logical. "If you keep calm and cool, nothing will get out of hand," he quoted. "That's good advice for any animal. Panicking may cause the creatures to panic as well. The calmer you are the calmer your ride will be." Too bad it was easier said than done.

Mischief took a deep breath, closed her eyes for a minute, then blew out. Then, she began to purr and relaxed her grip on the worn leather saddle. Muscles loose, she swayed in harmony with the beast's movement. She smiled. "Once you get used to the gait, you really can relax your grip and enjoy the ride."

Xander went into his own zone and followed her example. He didn't know if he'd taught her exceptionally well or if all her practice on that boogie board helped, but he did know he couldn't let her outshine him. After all, he was the teacher and she was the apprentice.

"Let yourself move around, but not too much and trust that you won't fall off," she murmured, then she resumed purring. He allowed her soothing sound to envelope him and on some level was surprised that the creature's gait had become oddly soothing, as well. The power of purrs was a magnificent thing. Following her example, he began purring, too. Peace enveloped him until the motion stopped and he nearly fell off.

His eyes snapped open to a wild valley with shades of vibrant green under a pale blue sky. Rumbling behind him came from an old concrete dam, which separated placid water from the cascade pouring into the shallow, rocky river. Where were they? His paws itched to consult his collar and confirm his location with the GPS function, but he didn't want to chance revealing his location to others.

"Best to get off here," the camel said. "Like I told you, the guy that hired me to transport this merchandise would get real angry if he knew I wasn't exclusive to him." The camel spat out a huge yellowish glob. Xander willed himself not to react.

"That's no problem," Xander said. "You've been most helpful and I wouldn't want to repay the favor by causing you problems."

"How much farther is the fort?" Mischief asked.

"You'll see it as soon as you round that bend." He nodded to an abrupt turn in the trail about fifty feet further. "That's why I needed to have you get off here. Once I'm on that leg, Ganas could see us."

Ganas?!? Had Hathor guided them to their quarry or was the name a coincidence?

Mischief suddenly launched herself upward, landing on a limb with grace. "We really, really appreciated your help," she said, "and I hope we meet again."

"And I really, really appreciated your purring," the camel said. "It made the trek much more pleasant than normal."

Xander also gave his thanks, then leaped up to join Mischief. As soon as the camel was out of sight, she whispurred, "Was he mocking me?"

Mocking her? That was her question instead of if Hathor had helped them find the correct Ganas? "What do you mean?"

"He said 'really, really', which is what I'd just said."

"Does it matter? As far as camels go, he was a very nice fellow and we seem to be making progress."

"Well, I was being sincere and I'd hate to think he thought I wasn't."

"Do you want to worry about that or focus on the fort and whoever or whatever might be there?"

She gulped. "I'd rather think about the camel because I'm afraid the Ganas he's taking that stuff to might be one of those Moreau misfits and they terrify me."

He knew exactly how she felt, but was not about to admit it. Moving from limb to limb, he purrposefully approached the section of path where the camel had disappeared. The thought that he'd been negligent not asking the fellow's name crossed his mind, but just as quickly he acknowledged that he was glad he hadn't since it also meant he hadn't given his name to the camel, who might have mentioned it to Ganas.

Mischief fearlessly leaped between trees and

quickly passed him, then she stopped and hunkered down in predator mode. When he joined her, he realized she'd chosen an ideal vantage point to watch the camel arrive at the ruins. A stone arch lying smashed on the ground seemed typical of the destruction. The crumbled mess barely resembled anything useful. Had word of mouth kept the name Mahuli Fort alive after war smashed the walls or had earthquakes torn apart the structure?

The camel passed a small group of humans, who were near what looked like an open Shiva temple and continued onward. Where was he going? Eventually, the camel stopped near the mouth of a cave, which he hadn't noticed and, as they watched, a dark grayish black creature emerged. Without talking, it began removing the supplies. If he'd had any doubts about the creature being the one he'd come halfway around the world looking for, they vanished as the dark creature, which appeared to be part ape; part cat moved the packages.

"Do you think it's just the two of them?" Mischief whispurred, her attention focused on the mouth of the cave. His fur hovered, when he realized that the creature, who was unloading the camel was handing each package to someone – or something – in the cave's shadows.

"Impossible to tell," he said. Not knowing how big the cave was, there was no way to know how many misfits could be inside, much less know if they were a threat to Catamondo or simply the miserable result of Chester's gene manipulation. The only way to find out was to get close enough to see and hear. He moved back down the branch, until he could jump to a better position to maneuver toward the cave.

Mischief was right on his tail. "Shouldn't we wait for dark?"

He paused, paw poised for his next jump. "Why?"

"We'd have an advantage in the dark."

"Are you sure?" He raised a brow. "Think about it. Do you know if monkeys can see well in the dark? For that matter, how can we know if their eye gene is monkey or cat?"

"You're positive they're Moreau Misfits, aren't you?"

"Positive? No. But I think there is a high probability."

She shivered.

"Are we done chatting?"

She nodded.

"Then come on, our best chance for getting closer without being noticed is now, while they're distracted with that camel and all those packages." He leaped to the next tree, then the next, next, next and next until it was close enough for his excellent hearing to pick up the sounds of movement and conversation. From that point on, he moved in stealth mode, finally arriving on a nice wide branch, which allowed him to see into the mouth of the cave, as well as listen to the high-pitched voices.

Mischief silently settled next to him, then placed her paw on top of his and tapped out, 'Do you think they always shriek like that?'

Since the bough of leaves, which camouflaged them from view by anything in the cave were swaying in the gentle breeze, Xander dipped his ear to indicate that he didn't know. However, if they always spoke in such ear-grating tones, it could certainly explain why they had been forced to live in isolation, instead of in the comforts of normal cat society.

'Don't put that there!" The screech felt like it stabbed through his ears.

"Why not?" The other one shrieked back.

"She said to put that stuff in the safest place and that's back there."

Xander glanced at Mischief through eyes, which were watering in sympathy with his abused ears. Her little calico face was scrunched in pain, but her attention hadn't wavered from the cave and her paw now lay on top of his own, as if she needed support to deal with the harsh voices. He put his other paw on top of hers and coded out that they needed to move father back.

He didn't need to tell her a second time.

They moved to a limb which was actually closer to the mouth of the cave, but it was off to the side and not in direct line of the high-pitched voices within. Even though they could not be seen by anyone inside the cave, Mischief put her paw over his and tapped out, 'Much better! My ears thank you."

He smiled at her, but kept his attention on their surroundings, because if the two creature inside were actually Ganas and Gandharvas and they were Moreau Misfits, which he could almost guarantee, there was every reason to believe things were not as rustic and harmless as they seemed. His paw itched to click on his collar and have it scan for subtle RF emissions. Not feeling free to use its technology was disconcerting, but if his worst suspicions were accurate, then it was wise to keep it turned off until he could either deal with the mess or chock everything up to a bad case of purr-a-noia.

=^.^=

Next to him, Mischief tensed. Xander glanced at her to see if there was actually danger coming from behind; her attention was riveted on a tree overhanging the path the camel had used.... a tree they had maneuvered through to escape detection. He narrowed his eyes, as he tried to see what had captured her attention, but only saw a grayish-brown squirrel scampering up the trunk. Still, unless he was mistaken – and he doubted that he was – Mischief's attention was riveted on that squirrel.

Why was she so interested in it?

Since there wasn't anything of interest going on inside the cave, he, too, watched the little squirrel as it reached a high limb, then ran away from the trunk. Didn't the creature have enough sense to slow down?

Instead, the squirrel gave a burst of speed and jumped!

Mischief gasped.

Dear Hathor, what had possessed the poor thing to do that? Didn't it realize jumping from well over one-hundred feet was suicide?

As he watched, the creature spread all four legs wide and instead of crashing to a horrible end, seemed to effortlessly glide to the bough they were hiding in. As it gracefully, landed, Mischief turned to him, her eyes were huge and he suspected his were, too.

The squirrel scooted headfirst down the tree to their branch, which was another thing he'd never figured out how to do. Backwards, going down, yes, but squirrels were obviously built a lot more differently than cats if they could not only scamper down headfirst, but also glide like a bird.

A shrill screech of anger distracted him from his thoughts. "What are you doing in MY TREE?!?" The squirrel demanded, as it barred its teeth and displayed its formidable claws.

"I was admiring how well you climb trees and fly," Mischief gushed, in a quiet voice. "I thought for certain that you were going to splat, but you flew instead! I didn't know that anything, except birds, could do that."

The squirrel's angry expression faltered. "Why are you in my tree?"

Mischief tilted an ear toward the cave. "There are a couple really weird cats in there... Have you seen them?"

The squirrel's fluffy tail swished, but it put its front paws on the branch in a non-threatening pose. "Yes, they like to climb my tree, too." It spit toward the cave. "But I don't think those things are cats."

"Why do you say that?" Mischief whispurred

"Can you or your furiend hang by your tail?"

"Beg pardon?"

Xander glanced toward the cave, half expecting to see something impossible, but nothing had changed and the only sounds from within were of eating.

"You heard me," the squirrel said. "They can hang from their tails, like monkeys, so I figure they're some weird sort of monkey, not cats."

"Well, that would explain a lot... Why do you say this is your tree?"

The squirrel's eyes narrowed. "Because I live here."

"OH! Oh, my! I'm so sorry! We didn't realize this tree was someone's home. We just wanted a good strong limb where we could watch that cave.... I'm sure we can find someplace else to sit."

"Well, that pair does need watching," the squirrel's voice was now as quiet as Mischief's.

When the animal agreed that they could stay in their position, as long as they kept away from its nest, Xander felt secure letting her continue to handle the unexpected situation, though he did keep one ear tuned to their conversation, the majority of his attention was on the discussion inside the cave. After arguing about eating pumpkins, which neither of them seemed familiar with, one of them popped open a can of Elegant Eats Pumpkin Purrfection, while the other one settled down for a nap. He wished he had that luxury, but someone needed to keep their claws in the situation.

A gentle breeze made the tree sway.

Was Hathor testing his resolve to stay awake?

He closed his eyes for a brief moment. Nearby, Mischief and the squirrel were whispurring about the difference between flying and gliding. When she asked if updrafts could be used to glide, the squirrel let out a shrill shriek of excitement, which nearly raised his sable coat.

He casually glanced back at the unlikely pair, who seemed to be on their way to becoming furiends. The squirrel was now standing on one foot, as it held out the opposing foot and arm, to display a wide area of furry skin that stretched from his wrist to his ankle. "It's my patagium," the creature said. "Just as good as any bird wing." He changed his stance to show he had one on his left side, too.

"But how do they work?"

The squirrel fluffed its impressive tail, then said, "I am from the family Sciuridae. Though we are not capable of actual flight in the way of birds or bats, we use our patagium to glide from one tree to another." He gestured toward the parachute-like membrane, then switched sides, again.

Mischief's brow wrinkled in thought as she extended her own arm and leg to one side, then the other. The difference in amount of skin that was available to catch air was obvious. "Do you just sort of slow fall when you glide or can you choose where you're going?"

The squirrel twirled its whiskers. "I can usually choose exactly which branch I want to land on."

"Usually?" Xander said.

The squirrel gave a little shiver, as if he'd forgotten about him, but he didn't lose any of his arrogance. "There are occasional wind issues."

"Updrafts?" Mischief asked.

"Those and downdrafts," the squirrel admitted.

"So you're pretty much at the mercy of wherever you get blown."

"No, no, no, no, no!" He turned so they had a better view of his long fluffy brown tail and patted it. "This provides stability in the air." He turned back to them. "When I'm gliding, I can control which limb – or whatever I wish to land on by the angle of my arms, legs and tail. It's different from walking and running, but not a lot. For instance, when I'm walking or running and want to stop, I simply don't move my legs, but when I'm gliding and I want to lose speed fast, I stick up my tail. It's a great brake!"

Mischief tried to copy the way his tail stuck up, but it looked pitiful by comparison.

A loud bang came from inside the cave. The squirrel's fur stood on end. "Gotta go!" the squirrel squeaked as he dashed to the trunk, then sprinted upward.

Meanwhile, Xander and Mischief hunkered down on the limb, alert for whatever might happen next. They didn't need to wait long before a shouting match erupted in the shadows. Then, with a reow, something flew out. After a bing and a bounce, a half-empty tin of Pumpkin Purrfection settled against a clump of grass, it's contents an orange gooey glob of deliciousness. His stomach gave a loud growl. Mischief looked at him, her eyes wide. He suspected he looked startled, too, but breakfast was a long time ago, so it was no wonder his stomach protested the waste of purrfectly prepared delectability.

From inside the cave, one of them hushed the other, then explained that he thought he'd heard something. Xander's stomach took the opportunity to growl again. They heard it, but only one of the misfits poked their shaggy gray head out of the cave to peer around.

Xander and Mischief stayed so still that a bird landed on their limb. Fortunately, his stomach kept quiet.

Eventually, the head disappeared and he heard rummaging sounds coming from inside. Mischief moved her paw to touch him and the startled bird flew away.

Again, a shaggy head poked out of the cave and peered around, then, with a roar, the misfit jumped toward the dripping can. A mouse shrieked as it fled. The monkey-cat began to chase it, but the rodent disappeared inside a crevasse. The predator peered into the broken rock, but didn't seem to be able to see the mouse. Xander's vantage point offered an excellent view of the clever mouse, which had somehow doubled back to the Elegant Eats can.

Mischief's paw tapped out, 'n o t v e r y s m a r t'. Judging by the creature's total focus on the crack, she was correct. He also suspected it didn't have particularly good hearing because the rodent was a noisy eater.

Suddenly, the mouse froze. It took Xander a moment to realize there was movement on the path that he and Mischief had arrived on. Unfortunately, he couldn't see what was coming, but he could hear bells. Lots of tiny, jingly bells that sounded just like Sari's collar. A moment later, a gust brought the scent of oranges.

Could Sari actually be here?

What were the odds?

A few moments later, Mumbai's Purrtector tapped the misfit on the shoulder and totally implicated herself as one of Chester's creations, by saying, "Gandharvas, what in the world are you doing?"

"Mouse."

"Forget the mouse. I've spent half the day hiking here. You can get the mouse later."

The creature tore its attention from the crack and focused on her. "You was supposed to come, tomorrow."

"I know, but my monitoring program showed that busybody was in this area and I was afraid he'd somehow managed to track you."

Mischief's paw stiffened on top of his and her claws involuntarily extended.

Gandharvas shook his shaggy head and even though he was at least twice as large as Sari, he acted like a penitent kitten, trying to please its mother. "I don't know why you're feared of him. He's just a plain old tom."

"The Kamikazi is a lot of things, but he isn't a plain old tom." Sari's bells chimed as she shook her head.

Ganas appeared in the mouth of the cave.

"When did you arrive?"

"Just now."

Ganas scratched his gray head, leaving orangish streaks. "Does this mean we need to dump the virus in the water early?"

"How come you're feared on that tom cat and a kitten?" Gandharvas demanded. "There be three of us and only two of them. You think we can't lick and old tom and a baby?"

"I think we can do things smarter than Chester and not get caught," Sari said.

"You think dumping that virus will fix everything." Gandharvas tilted his head to one side. "If'n that be so, how come you didn't do it, like the boss-tom told you when you first got it?"

"You know why," Ganas turning his full attention to his vat-mate. "We were keeping a low profile... Once Chester was dead, we didn't know if killing more cats would be in our best interests or not." His long sinewy tail whipped from side to side like a black tufted whip. "But now that we know that they know we're alive, we might as well use the stuff and get back at the jerks that called us names."

"And threw rocks." Gandharvas placed his paw over his forehead. "Don't be forgetting the rocks."

Xander focused his attention on Gandharvas' head and realized the tom's right ear was scarred and torn. Looking as close as possible without his collar, he also thought the fur laid in a pattern, which indicated that broken bones had healed beneath. A head fracture could explain why Gandharvas' speech seemed labored and slow compared to Ganas. While he was sorry that other cats had been so nasty to the strange-looking pair, he also understood why they were difficult to accept and others felt the need to chase them away.

Mischief's paw tapped out a question about if he thought they might have turned into decent toms if they had gone to Master Mahat's orphanage, instead of live on their own. It was a good question, but there was no way to know... and no way to answer her without moving, which could attract attention.

Below them, the discussion about releasing the virus raged. Fortunately, without the cave to magnify their voices, Ganas and Gandharvas' voices didn't hurt his ears as much. And it was very handy to know what they intended to do.

A faint sound behind them diverted his attention. So while Mischief continued to watch Sari and the two misfits, his gaze searched the path, rocks and trees for a clue to the sound. Things were strangely silent in one tree, so he focused his attention there and waited.

And waited.

He heard Sari and at least one other go back inside the cave. Risking a glance, he determined that all three were inside, but that didn't mean they could afford doing anything that could attract attention. If Sari had managed to install a monitoring program on his collar, without him noticing, what other technology had she gotten her claws on?

Finally, a breeze rippled the leaves and he caught a glimpse of white tail tip.

Turning his attention forward, he tightened his muscles in the paw, which Mischief was touching and coded that Merlin had arrived. Aside from enlarged pupils, she managed to control her body, so she didn't yelp with excitement or dash off to greet him. Their location safe, for the moment, Xander's tension lessened.

=^.^=

As the waxing moon rose, Merlin joined them on their limb and whispurred, "You chose a better position than I did."

Mischief put her free front paw on his and tapped out a warning to be quiet, the movement of her toes would have been undetectable, if he hadn't known what she planned to do. Merlin's ears perked, as he, too, got the message, then, he frowned, so Mischief tapped out that to respond, he could tense and untense his paws. Eyes bright with understanding, Merlin did just that. It took a few shorts and longs before Xander noticed that Mischief's covering paw moved slightly upward when Merlin's paw tensed.

Mischief's paw on top of his own began to tap out what Merlin had told her.

Xander lowered an ear, which was her signal to be quiet. When she immediately complied, he then coded to her how he had read the tiny movements and that she was smart to make the assumption that Sari had some sort of technology capable of monitoring them. She inhaled, obviously very impressed with his attention to detail. It took a lot of self control not to twirl his whiskers.

When Mischief finished relaying his thoughts to Merlin, his fluffy white friend coded a question asking if he'd seen any sign of potential technology.

Aside from the small solar panel, no, but they hadn't done a complete reconnaissance.

While relaying his response, Mischief added that if she'd set up the cave as a hideout, she would have put up cameras and heat detectors to watch the approach to the cave, but before she could elaborate, Sari jingled her way out of the cave and strolled majestically down the path. Why was she returning so quickly?

Did she know Merlin had followed her?

If he followed her, would she lead him into a trap?

More scraping and shuffling drew his attention back to the cave, where Gandharvas, then Ganas emerged, each dragging a dirty burlap bag behind them.

Even though they were making so much noise that a brass band could have marched behind them unnoticed, Xander, Merlin and Mischief moved as quietly through the boughs as possible, frequently pausing to sniff the breeze and look for unexpected surveillance.

# Chapter 11

As Sari sashayed onto the moonlit dam, which held Mumbai's water supply captive, her steps kept beat to the rock and roll music, which the calm water magnified. Gandharvas and Ganas sat down under a pine tree, apparently unwilling to take another step. Xander watched with interest as Sari realized she was alone. Whirling around, she stomped back to the defiant pair.

"She looks angry," Mischief whispurred, her whiskers tickling his ear.

He inclined his head in agreement. Despite the fact that Gandharvas and Ganas were each at least double Sari's size, they acted more defensive the closer she got.

"Wish someone would turn off that music," Merlin muttered.

"True," Xander said. It would be nice to hear

what she was snarling at her cohorts. Nicer still, if she mentioned what they planned to do, so he would have a better idea how to stop her.

Mischief tilted her head toward a nearby clearing. "Music is from there, by that fire." She sniffed the air. "Smells like fried fish."

Apparently the other three had gotten a whiff, too, because Gandharvas and Ganas abruptly got up, but instead of doing what Sari wanted, they left their filthy bags under the pine tree and began trotting toward a flickering light. He was fairly certain their interest was in the food, not the music. When it became obvious that the other two wouldn't turn around, no matter how loud she yowled at their tufted tails, Sari stomped after them.

As soon as she disappeared into the underbrush, Xander and Merlin dashed out and each grabbed one of the bags. Since they were much lighter than the misfits had made them look, they hauled the bags into the woods. After the bags were well hidden, they went in the direction the other three had taken.

The closer they got to the music, the stronger the delightful aroma of food. His stomach growled in anticipation. To take his mind off this empty tummy, he tried to recall what he'd heard of this area. If memory served – and it usually did – Tansa Wildlife Sanctuary bordered the lake, which the dam created. Xander sniffed the air, wondering if he might be able to smell panther, wild boar, cheetah, antelope, jackal, or hyena... would he even know what he was smelling if he did catch the scent of one? Since Tansa Lake had been a water source for wildlife for centuries, he also took his time scanning the shoreline and determined that the flickering light was a bonfire on the beach. Strangely, he didn't see anyone sitting around it. Had some humans been inconsiderate enough to leave the potential hazard unattended?

There was a splash followed by laughter, which suggested that whoever had built the fire was taking a moonlight swim. If the three Moreau Misfits hadn't been skulking around it, he would have been tempted to grab a snack.

Unfortunately, the timing wasn't quite right for that.

Since they didn't want to be burdened with the bags and didn't want them easily found, he and Merlin had climbed high in a couple tree then secured the bags. If they were lucky, they would have an opportunity to destroy the bags in the fire, before the night was over.

The silhouettes of Gandharvas and Ganas looked black against the flames. Were they arguing with Sari about food or how to distribute the virus?

The closer they approached to the fire, the louder the music became, which was a good thing, since the stronger the scent of food became, the more his tummy growled. Merlin and Mischief, both gave him surprised looks, but they were polite enough not to say anything.

Merlin led the way to a tall, conical tree, which had branches over the fire. It would offer an excellent view of Sari, Gandharvas and Ganas chowing down on the human's leftovers. Since the Moreaus were in front of the fire, it was difficult to see the humans splashing in the lake. Fortunately, he could keep track of their shrieks of laughter, despite the loud music. Unfortunately, due to all the noise clutter, it was difficult to hear what the three Moreau misfits were saying, particularly since they were talking with their mouths full, but he had the impression that Sari wanted to poison Mumbai's water supply because she hated the stupid, annoying cats she had to deal with, while the other two apparently wanted to poison a water hole where a certain tribe of monkeys drank.

Xander closed his eyes in the hopes that his stomach wouldn't growl if he couldn't see the fish, but he could still smell it. In fact, he salivated so much he needed to swallow, so he focused on the nearby conversation.

"Just look at her smug expression," Mischief muttered. "I'd love to get my paws on her and make her as sorry as her name sounds."

Merlin chuckled, then asked, "Are you putting dibs on her?"

It didn't take Mischief long to answer. "Well, there are three of them and three of us and not all toms like to fight girls, so yes, I am putting dibs on her!"

"Works for me," Merlin said, "But are you sure you want her and not the one with the torn ear? He's clumsy."

"Are you suggesting that I can't take her?"

"Well, she is at least double your weight and she has had Purrtector combat training."

"And that klutz is at least twenty to twenty-five

pounds. So, how come you think I can take him and not that sorry excuse of a Purrtector?"

"If you want to deal with her, she's yours," Xander said. He turned toward Merlin. "I've never had Purrtector combat training, either, but I've been teaching her everything I learned on the Kickboxing Circuit since she was a month old."

Merlin squinted at Mischief, who tried to puff up and look as big as possible. "You're how old?"

"Almost eight months."

As Merlin and Mischief whispurred back and forth, Xander nudged them toward the pine tree's trunk, then, he moved to the dark side and began climbing. In no time, he heard the other two stop squabbling and start ascending the trunk, too. About thirty feet up, he found a nice sturdy branch with an ideal view of the fire. Settling onto a crook in it, he closed his eyes and focused his attention on the night sounds beneath the blaring music.

"Have you nodded off?" Merlin asked.

"Nope, just purrtecting my night vision from being compromised by the fire. Besides, when I'm not distracted, I can better focus on what I hear and I think the humans are done swimming."

After a short pause, Merlin said, "I think you're correct... It should be interesting when they spot those three eating their fish."

Xander's stomach gave a huge roar.

Sounds of running paws came from below, then, he heard claws speed-climbing the trunk of the tree they were hiding in. Dear Hathor, this was not good at all!

His stomach growled again.

The sounds of approaching claws stopped about ten feet below and a tense silence ensued. Xander's claws sank into the rough bark as he held his breath and prayed that his stomach wouldn't give their location away.

At the bonfire, the humans laughed and joked as they collected their things, then leaving the fire burning, they headed down the path to the receding beat of their music.

Soon, the loudest sound was the crackling of the flames.

Xander quietly inhaled and held his breath as he counted to ten.

After several more minutes of peace and quiet, the bough below lurched and Sari whispurred, "Stop that!"

There was a low growl, but the sound of movement ceased, though the limb continued to sway. A pinecone landed on the ground, then bounced into the flames. Moments later it popped.

Ganas and Gandharvas shrieked.

"Shut up you fools," Sari snarled.

In the distance, car doors slammed, then a motor started. Xander closed his eyes just in time to avoid the headlights. Though Merlin and Mischief didn't make a sound, from below, there were howls of being blinded.

"I told you idiots to shut up!"

"B-b-b-but I'm blind!"

"Serves you right for being stupid enough to have your eyes open," Sari snarled. When the other two began to whine, she added, "I'm outta here." Hearing the sounds of movement, Xander peeked downward to see a pair of bright lime-green eyes moving past two pairs of luminous red eyes, as Sari made her way toward the trunk.

Next to him, Merlin inhaled sharply. Xander felt his fur stand at attention, but Mischief was resolutely marching toward the tree's trunk, apparently determined that no one come between her and her confrontation with Sari.

What in the snake pit of inferno damnation had glowing red eyes? Had Chester somehow managed to cross Ganas and Gandharvas with demons? Worse, he'd never seen florescent lime green eyes in all his life.

Should he stop Mischief?

Before he could make up his mind, Mischief disappeared around the far side of the pine's trunk and began her descent. Something tickled his ear, though tempted to smack it, he quickly recognized the feel of whiskers. Merlin leaned close enough so he could feel his breath tickle his ear. "Does she know not to go down nose first?"

Xander nodded, then whispurred to Merlin, "She might not spend a lot of time in trees, but she's an expert when it comes to climbing the mast... you know how much harder those are."

Merlin made a soft, strangled sound, which Xander interpreted as muffled laughter. A moment later, he whispurred, "Do you think we should stay up here or confront that pair when they're still blinking."

"I was about to head down." He tipped an ear toward Sari, who was slipping and sliding as she tried to climb down the trunk nose first. "Was distracted by the show."

"For the kid's sake, I hope her fighting skills are as incompetent as her tree ones."

Xander did, too.

With no reason to continue procrastinating and every reason to confront Ganas and Gandharvas, so he could tie up the problem before they contaminated the water with bird flu, he resolutely headed toward the trunk and then expertly descended to the limb they were on.

With a shriek and a plop, Sari landed face first on the ground. A spit second later, Mischief shot down on top of her and tried to pin her larger foe. Sari screamed an obscenity and threw Mischief off, the closest Moreau misfit, shrieked and leaped off the branch, then swung by its tail. The other misfit howled in terror and clung to the branch with all fours plus its tail.

Xander didn't have the luxury of watching Mischief as the chaos broke loose because he dove onto the back of the hanging one. Merlin let out a warwhoop as he flew downward, landing on the back of the cowering one, like a white shroud.

The next few moments were a blur because the one he had his claws in tried to escape by swinging through the limbs by its tail. Xander didn't know if the creature was clumsy, still blind from the lights or didn't know how to compensate for the extra sixteen pounds of Siamese on his back, but it was the craziest trip he'd ever made through a tree.

By the time they crashed to the ground, Mischief and Sari were gone. Sounds of pleading and crying were coming from above. Instead of run, Gandharvas turned and tried to fight him. The creature was as incompetent at kickboxing as he was at catching mice. Purrhaps Merlin was correct and he should have told Mischief to deal with the klutz.

Xander easily evaded Gandharvas, so the big guy kept kicking and clawing the air, which made him angrier and angrier.

In the distance, he heard Mischief and Sari screaming at each other. He had the distinct impression that Sari was climbing another tree and Mischief had her by the tail. If he hadn't needed to deal with Gandharvas, he would have liked to see that.

From above, a branch shook loose two more pinecones as Merlin and Ganas descended. Not taking his attention off Gandharvas' eyes, Xander kicked a cone into the flames. A few moments, later, the cone popped, sending sparks over his opponent's fur. Gandharvas shrieked, as if he'd been shot.

Ganas screeched.

Xander kicked Gandharvas in the throat, effectively both cutting off his breath and knocking him down. Before the dust settled, he was on top of the gasping creature, pinning him so he couldn't get away. "What were you planning to do with the toxin?" He demanded.

Gandharvas spit at him.

Xander extended one paw's claws and gave the creature a good close look at them. "Do I need to repeat myself?" He inched his shives closer to tender flesh.

"Sari wanted to make the cats in Mumbai sick 'cause she didn't figure they respected her."

"Keep going."

"It was all her idea!"

"Aren't you forgetting about what you and your vat mate wanted to do?"

"How'd you know about that?"

Xander flexed his paw.

Gandharvas quickly added, "We wanted to get even with a troop of macaques 'cause they hated us. Threw sh-"

His paw remained steady, despite his welling anger. "You felt that returning an insult with death was fair?"

"It was just the flu."

Just the flu?!? "Are you aware that everyone, including Chester, who has been exposed to it is dead?"

'That's a lie!"

"That's the truth and if you read *The Daily Mews* you'd know it."

"What's *The Daily Mews*?"

Having never met someone that didn't know that, he blinked several times. "Do you know what a newspaper is?"

Gandharvas shook his head.

"Did anyone ever teach you to read?" He shook his head, again. Xander scratched his ear. "Who raised you?"

"Me 'n' Ganas been alone since we can remember. 'Course Ms. Sari come by a lot... at least at first, but then she wanted to better herself. 'N' she done real good, 'cause she be smart."

"If I get off of you, will you sit and talk with Merlin and I, instead of try and fight us?"

"Yous wants to talk? Sari said you and the little one wanted to kill me 'n' Ganas."

"My goal was find you and your vat mate and determine if you were a threat to Catamondo."

"Who's dat?"

"Not a who, a what.... Hathor herself organized cats thousands of years ago, so domestic or feral, purebred or wild, every cat abides by a set of rules for conduct." Xander gracefully moved off Gandharvas and sat down. Despite his confidence that the creature wasn't an immediate threat, a lifetime of training made him choose an easily defensible position. As Gandharvas clumsily struggled to sit up, he risked a glance around for Mischief and Merlin. Though no one else was in sight, he could hear Merlin having a similar conversation with Ganas and farther away, Sari was still trying to get away from Mischief... He wished her luck with that, after all he'd been trying to do that since she was just a month old and she was still stuck to him like an uncompromising burr. While that had turned out well for him, he doubted it would for Sari.

As the moon rose, an ear-splitting shriek, accompanied by the sound of branches cracking echoed over the lake. For a moment, his fur tried to stand on end, but he controlled it. Gandharvas wasn't so disciplined, so he visibly doubled his already impressive size. Next, he heard a hard smack, a moment later, a splash.

"What was that?"

"Sounded like something fell out of a tree."

"So it wasn't something dying or anything bad?"

"Don't know." He thought it sounded like Sari and Mischief had fallen, but since Gandharvas hadn't asked, he didn't see the need to volunteer that information. Confident that Hathor would protect his apprentice, Xander settled down to learn everything he could from Gandharvas.

By the time the first light of dawn began to gleam on the lake's surface, he and Merlin had successfully burned the toxin and knew that Sari had been the brains, while Ganas and Gandharvas were little more than uneducated pawns.

Merlin frowned. "So, what do we do with them?"

"Wish I knew." After all, it wasn't a clear case of intentional misdeeds. "What they really need is guidance, understanding and education."

"Purrhaps Master Mahat could teach them," Mischief said, from behind him.

Xander whirled around. His apprentice got a smug look, knowing that she'd managed to sneak up on him, but the most shocking part was that her fur was spiked up in every direction and her whites were streaked with rainbow colors. He blinked, hoping it was a trick of the light. It wasn't.

"What happened to you?"

She shrugged. "I taught Sari what a sorry soul she was."

"And the pink, green and purple splotches?" Merlin asked.

"Remember those ribbons I had tied on my collar?" They both nodded. "Well, the dye wasn't very good." To emphasize her remark, she hooked a claw in a wrinkled, bedraggled greenish strip and yanked it off her collar. He hoped the gray stain on her collar could be cleaned off.

"Where's Ms. Sari?" Ganas asked.

Mischief bit her lower lip and looked toward the dam. "I'm not really sure, but her collar is here." With a shimmy and a wiggle, she slid it off her waist. "I thought it might have information."

"Good thinking!" Merlin said.

"Why are you avoiding telling us what you did to Sari?" Xander asked. "You didn't kill her, did you?"

"Of course not!"

When she didn't continue, he added, "The whole story, please."

Mischief frowned. "I'm not exactly sure where to begin... and to be honest, I'm not a hundred percent sure what happened in a couple spots." Xander motioned for her to continue. "Well, I jumped on her and she flipped me and I almost landed in the fire, but I jumped back at her, except she was running away, so I missed. There was a lot of noise up by you, so I figured you were dealing with them... by the way, how come they aren't tied up or something?"

"They are cooperating and shall be dealt with appropriately." Hearing that, Ganas seemed to shrink inside his matted, long gray fur. Again, he motioned for Mischief to continue.

"Well, she started getting tired, so she decided to climb a tree." She scratched her ear, which left muddy streaks. "I guess she figured she'd lose me, but she's a really, really bad climber, so it was super easy to catch her."

"Bit her tail didn't you?" Merlin asked.

"How'd you know?" He wiggled his ears. "Yeah, I did, but she kept on trying to climb, so I sort of used my weight to hang onto her and it got too hard to go up, so she decided to go out on a limb... Can you believe she was dumb enough to choose a dead branch?"

Xander scratched his head, then reminded himself that Sari probably had never had much chance to climb trees, at least not since she'd moved into Catamondo's society.

"So, the branch broke," Merlin said.

"Yes it did! And I let go of her when she screamed. Would you believe that she didn't even know how to fall right?" Xander nodded. "I'm not sure what she did, but it wasn't smart. Meanwhile, I did the flying squirrel thing, so I could glide far enough to land in deep water."

"What's a flying squirrel thing?" Gandharvas asked.

"Basically, you spread out as flat as possible and use your tail as a rudder," Xander said.

Mischief nodded. "And it worked great! I think Sari must have hit a rock face first, but I was concentrating on where to land, not what she was doing." Again, she scratched her ear. "For certain, by the time I swam to her, she was half knocked out, plus one eye and her nose was real bloody."

"I'd have liked to see that," Ganas said,

What sort of bloodthirsty creature was he?

Mischief looked at the general area of the lake where he'd heard the crash. "I didn't know what would happen, so I quickly grabbed her collar, so we could..." She looked from Gandharvas to Ganas. "Um, about the time I was squeezing into it, she came around and attacked me. But, again, she didn't think first because all that she managed to do was knock us both into the lake."

"I thought you said you fell into the lake," Gandharvas said.

"I did. She landed on a rock that was within jumping distance of the shore. When I swam back, I needed to get on the rock so I could get her collar off." She looked at the calm water, glowing in the morning sun. "That looks calm as all get out, but a current took her to the dam and it was pretty clear that she couldn't swim any better than she could land properly."

"And you?" Merlin asked.

"Oh, I got out, again, then tracked her from the shore. Once the dam spit her out, I figured I could grab her, but I was wrong."

"She never made it through?" Xander asked.

"Oh, she did and I would have grabbed her, except Spooky Powac beat me to her and there was no way I was going to fight him for her."

Gandharvas and Ganas both shivered at the name.

"Who is Spooky Powac?" Xander asked.

"He be a monstrous big black cat!" Ganas wailed.

"He's a demon!" Gandharvas howled.

"Lord Spooky PoWAC is a panther and Purrtector of Wild Asian Cats," Merlin said. "Lord Purr has mentioned him being a bit bloodthirsty, but fair. His rank is equivalent to Continental Purrtector. Purr said Spooky was a good tom, but tended to get riled up about the rights of wild animals and how humans continue to encroach on their ancestral grounds."

"Continental Purrtector!" Mischief echoed, as she sat with a plot. "I knew he acted official, but wow!...He was at least seven feet long and said Sari would get Divine Justice for her crimes – and intended crimes against all animals... Even though he didn't have a collar or anything to show authority, I believed him, when he told me he'd keep in touch, then he grabbed Sari by the scruff, like she was a blind baby or something and disappeared into the forest... I didn't know what else to do, so I came back here." She looked from Gandharvas to Ganas. "Do you think Mr. Spooky wants to deal with them, too?"

The Moreau misfits howled in fright and threw themselves face-first onto the ground.

# *C*hapter 12

*X*ander peered from Gandharvas to Ganas. Both of them looked like they were trying to merge with the earth. Would Lord Spooky PoWAC take this pair off his paws? Even if he would, was that the right thing to do? While Sari had proven herself to be guilty, Gandharvas and Ganas were more like ignorant kittens who had been given a poor example to follow and bad advice. He sighed. "Something tells me that if he'd wanted this pair, he'd have grabbed them a long time ago."

While the Moreau misfits continued to hug the ground, Merlin murmured in agreement, "True, so we're still stuck in the middle of nowhere with a pair who've broken several of Hathor's laws."

"B-b-b-but what laws did we broke?" Gandharvas asked.

Where should he begin?

"Well, most recently, you were planning to help that sorry excuse of a Purrtector kill off all sorts of cats, plants and any animal who drank the poisoned water," Mischief snarled.

Ganas raised his tear and dirt streaked face. "She said it'd only make 'em sick!"

"The tan one says she lied and it was all over some news thingy," Gandharvas said.

Xander scratched his ear. "Seems to me that a big part of our current problem is that these two -"

"We knows wes dumb," Gandharvas said.

Ganas nodded, causing a tear to drip off his cheek. "She tol' us dat all de time."

"I was going to say uneducated," Xander said. He cleared his throat, when he and Merlin had begun talking about coming to India and tracking down this pair, he'd never expected to feel pity for them.

"We came here to figure out if there was an epidemic and if it was a coincidence that an illness with similar symptoms sprang up in this area." Mischief's tail swished. "The way I see it, we've answered that, Sari is being dealt with, we've found these two, so our job is done and now we can go surfing!" She smiled at Merlin.

"True, but we still need to tie up loose ends," Xander said.

Merlin moved to the shoreline and tapped his collar. Even though he was speaking softly, it was soon evident that he was talking with Lord Purr.

Mischief looked from Merlin to him, her expression angry. "How come he gets to use his collar and we can't?"

"Now that Sari is no longer a threat, it's probably safe to turn ours on, too."

No sooner was the thought out of his mouth, but they both clicked on their collars. As soon as his finished its initial program load, he was notified that he had twenty-six-thousand-seventy-six unread emails, Nineteen-hundred-fifty-nine voice mails and Two-thousand-thirteen Skype messages. Dear Hathor, his collar had been turned off for less than twenty-four hours, what catastrophe had happened while he was avoiding electronic tracking, that had caused such a tidal wave of communication?

Mischief fiddled with her collar. "I don't think this is as water-proof as they said."

"What's the problem?"

Eyes wide, she looked up at him, her tufted, rainbow streaked fur looked even more comical in the strengthening light of day. "The Council wants me to report to them." Her voice squeaked.

Why would they want that? The Council never contacted subordinates. He quickly scanned through who had been trying to communicate with him and realized that The Council had requested that he report to them, as well. Xander swallowed the lump trying to grow in his throat. "They want to speak to me, too."

Mischief wailed. "Am I in trouble because I let Mr. Spooky take Sari?"

Xander shook his head. "I don't know what they want, but I can assure you it won't be about that."

"How can you know?"

"Because only Spooky and the five of us know about that."

"Oh." She visibly relaxed. "Well, I guess I'd better get it over with." She raised her paw.

"Email or voice message, but don't Skype."

"And why not?"

"Because you look like a spiked rainbow." Xander nodded toward the lake. "Go check out your reflection and groom as best you can, while I respond to them."

"You'd better take some of your own advice... you've got pine needles and bark stuck to the top of your head and your back."

As they finished grooming their fur, Merlin finally got done with his conference call. "Purr says these toms are in his country and he'll see to it that they get properly integrated."

"What's in-tea-grated mean?" Ganas howled in fright.

"It means that Master Mahat and Ms. Kaberi have volunteered to take you in and teach you how to be proper cats," Merlin said. "It also means that if you don't do your best to learn and fit into Catamondo society that you'll be turned over to Spooky. Got it?"

Both Moreau creations groveled their agreement.

Merlin turned to him. "Hurry up and make your conference call with The Council."

Xander frowned. "How'd you know about that?"

"Just talked to Purr, among other things." Merlin's expression suggested that he knew a great deal more than he was saying.

"Is this bad?" Mischief asked.

Merlin's ear twitched. "I don't think so, but who knows what you two will think."

No matter how hard they pushed, Merlin refused to say another word. No matter how hard she tried, Mischief couldn't remove all the pastel purple stains from her fur. Figuring that it was best to get whatever he dreaded over and done, Xander took a deep breath than typed in the Council's code. He'd barely exhaled his anxiety when Lord Purr connected. "Kamakazi, my furiend, so glad to see you! And you, too Ms. Mischief." He squinted at her. "Did my mate have you test our shampoo? You look a bit lavender."

Mischief shook her head. "No on the shampoo... Am I in trouble or something? I mean, I've never heard of anyone my age getting summoned to speak to The Council."

Lord Purrmetheus' laugh was so loud that it seemed to echo over the lake. "On the contrary, if half of what Frazer just reported is fact, then I think it's safe to say that we are all very impressed with you!"

"What'd Frazer report?" An unknown voice asked. Lord Purrmetheus waited until everyone was logged onto the conference call before he told them about Sari's situation, Gandharvas and Ganas' capture and his plans to deal with the later pair. Many well dones echoed over the connection.

"Now," said Lord Purr, as he took control, "let me begin by telling Kamikazi that Lady Mitzi has put in her resignation letter because of health issues." Xander noticed that Merlin didn't seem surprised to hear this. "Furthermore, due to his exemplary purrformance taking care of this Moreau business, we've unanimously appointed you, Kamikazi, to be our acting Purrsident."

Xander sat down hard. Of all the things he'd imagined The Council wanting to speak to him about, he had never imagined such a statement.

Merlin head-butted him. "Congrats, Pal!"

As he sat in shock, Lord Purrmetheus continued to tell them that The Council now understood how important having Sea Purrtectors was and that it was too huge a Purrtectorate for one cat, so Merlin had agreed to become the Pacific Purrtector and despite her age, Mischief would become the Acting Atlantic Purrtector.

Mischief smiled bigger than he'd imagined possible. "How about we celebrate by surfing at Diego Garcia Island?"

Merlin's smile widened.

Xander groaned.


### THE END ###

I hope you enjoyed *Me-YEOW!*. If so, please leave a review on the book's product page. Reviews are very important to authors, so they are greatly appreciated.


Thank you!

# $O$ther Books by Jeanne Foguth

**Sci-Fantasy:**

*Kazza's Chatterre Trilogy*

## *Star Bridge*

Nimri, an herbal healer and Chatterer's new Keeper of the Peace, must safeguard her tribe from their bitter rivals. To do this, she must find her 'magic core'.

Many light years away, Colonel Larwin Atano, an elite Guerreterre Shadow Warrior, fights to save his intergalactic star-fighter. Despite all efforts, he crashes.

Larwin perceives Chatterre's resources as a means to gain power and prestige and views the planet's inhabitants as a minor inconvenience.

Nimri believes Larwin is a supernatural Guardian, who will protect her tribe from their rivals.

Who will survive the coming conflict?

## *Thunder Moon*

Thunder Cartwright dreams that madrox (dragons) will invade Chatterre and destroy his world unless the star bridge is closed.

Raine, a Kalamaran Dragon Shepard, must

catch a rogue mooncalf and return it to the herd or face possible death.

Who will will win and who will die?

## *Fire Island*

Tem-aki Atano fell through a rift, when the star bridge was destroyed and must find a way to survive on an island, which worships destructive madrox (dragons).

Cameron O'Ryan, must figure out if legend and reality have things in common or merely are stories told to children.

Meanwhile three dragon eggs are hatching... Will they destroy the island and everyone living on it? Or can they be controlled?

**Fantasy**

*Xander's Sea Purrtection Files:*

## *Latitudes and Cattitudes*

~ A prequel to the Sea Purrtector Files ~

This short prequel to the Sea Purrtector Files centers on Xander de Hunter when he is a rising star on Catamondo's kick-boxing circuit, with dreams of becoming a Purrtector.

After a match in Seattle, he is asked to help find Cha-Cha, a white Norwegian beauty, who is missing.

With Merlin's assistance, they follow Cha-Cha's trail into the Puget Sound where Xander must face his biggest fear – water.

## The Red Claw

Dame Esmeralda, the Purrsident's littermate, has been catnapped. Xander de Hunter, Catamondo's Sea Purrtector hurries to Jamaica to help rescue her, even though Jamaica is one of Dogdom's strongholds.

Could this be a trap?

## Purr-a-noia

Catamondo and Dogdom's peace treaty is in jeopardy. In Haiti, witchcraft and voodoo seem to be involved in a plot to hex the Purrsident.

Will Xander be able to restore the peace?

## The Vi-Purrs

The Daily Mews reports continued violence in the Dominican Republic Purrtectorate.

Xander discovers that the Moreau situation is still affecting the ability of Catamondo to purrtect cats. Worse, the office of the Dominican Republic's Purrtector seems to be involved.

Will Xander be able to restore peace?

## *Me-YEOW!*

There is an epidemic in Mumbai, India, where Chester Moreau first had problems with Catamondo. Coincidence? The Purrtector Council does not think so. Xander and Mischief fly to Mumbai, where they will meet Merlin and hope to sort out the problems.

Will Catamondo prevail or will Chester have his final revenge?

## Contemporary Suspense/Romance

## *Deadly Rumors*

Kelsey MacLennan and Devlin Doran both want to make the world better.

Doran believes the rumors about the MacLennans dealing drugs, so his goal is to bring them down.

Kelsey MacLennan wants to make the world better, but her senatorial political campaign turns deadly and rumors abound, when the incumbent must win or be killed by his backers. Devlin Doran's younger sister died of an overdose, so his goal is to prosecute pushers. Rumors abound that the MacLennans are high in the local drug network and he is targeting Kelsey MacLennan.

Will they be able to separate fact from fiction or will the rumors be deadly?

## *Fatal Attractions*

Ariel and Tempest Danner have escaped Tempest's homicidal father for the sixth time in five years. Armed with new identities and disguises, they are determined that Fairbanks, Alaska will be a sanctuary where they can live in peace.

Stone O'Banyon, their new landlord, has been divorced for three years. All his energy is focused on his job and Dolly, who would never hurt him.

The last thing Ariel needs or wants is the attraction she feels for another tall, dark man, who seems hard as the granite he is named for, but the fascination will not go away. Stone isn't any happier with his obsessive thoughts concerning Ariel.

Things seem calm, then Ariel and Tempest catch sight of the man they had hoped they would never encounter and things turn fatal...again.

## *Passion's Fire*

Prior to the blaze that killed her husband, Jacqueline Cardew believed her husband wrote the "fiery messages' she received. Now she finds a new note inside her locked house. Jacqueline suspects her faceless stalker murdered Adam and she is next. She flees north, where she joins Link Gavallan's group on a two week long Alaskan wilderness canoe trip. As they float down the desolate river, she receives another message…

Instead of finding a sanctuary, has she made it easier for her stalker to trap her?

# Connect with Jeanne Foguth

Though Jeanne began her career technical writing, her love of romantic-suspense, whether it be present, future or in an unknown galaxy inspired her to write the novels she wanted to find in bookstores. Since marrying, Jeanne and her husband have lived from the arctic to the tropics, as well as from yacht to off-grid mountain home. She loves using vivid colors and flowing shapes in her oil paintings as well as creating edible landscapes. She recently finished preparing previously-published novels for their digital debut and is now working on new stories.

*You can always find out what she is working on and/or contact her at:*

*Her blog: http://foguth.wordpress.com*

*Her web-home: http://www.jeannefoguth.com/*

*Facebook:*
*https://www.facebook.com/jeannefoguth*

OR follow on Twitter @JeanneFoguth

www.ingramcontent.com/pod-product-compliance
Lightning Source LLC
Chambersburg PA
CBHW071233130626
46556CB00003B/997